Marvellous.

By Cynical J.

intro

Before we start with are strange story, (well, not really a story, more like the complete and utter truth) let's get some facts straight, superheroes and comic book heroes truly do walk the earth. (Not all of them of course, that would be ridiculous, because some of them go beyond the boundaries of what we imagine to be possible, and once Stan started to write about them, the comic book world opened up and spread like a virus, new writers were popping up every day dreaming up fantastic new heroes.) Still there are many real comic book heroes and superheroes and they have been here for centuries. Nobody knows how long, some of them have a vague idea of which planets and different universes they come from; some of them know they are earth creatures evolved or shaped over the millennium from different creatures that no longer roam the earth. Some of them acquired their abilities from freak accidents or lab experiments. A few examples of all these scenarios would be the incredible hulk, superman, and the invisible man, the hulk is from planet hulk which is in a completely different universe to our own, we cannot see this universe and they cannot see ours for we are billions of light years apart; the hurtling light from the edge of our own universe has not yet reached the hurtling light from the edge of their universe, though they are on a collision course. The hulk arrived on earth by falling through a freak worm hole that joined both universes; the poor creature was just in the wrong place at the wrong time. Superman on the other hand, is actually from the planet krypton which is in our universe and came to earth in the way we all know, his planet is now gone and he is the last of his race, and Last but not least there's the invisible man, who back in the sixteenth century had a freak accident in a lab and that's that. So, each individual superhero has a tale of their own on how they came to be on earth or how they evolved on earth. These creatures wonder our globe, some of them are good and some of them are bad, living their lives as they will. At some time in the early sixteenth century they began to wander to the new land; some would call it America. As time went by they would cross paths with one another, some liking each other and some not, this inevitably lead to the concept of good and bad. They started to congregate or congeal and to form groups when they felt a connection to each other. The bad or nasty minded of these beings hated the human race because they were barbaric. Once or twice some of these beings were caught or seen by the humans, they were hunted down, tortured, hung, chopped to pieces, drowned or burnt at the stake because the humans did not understand them or their strange anatomy. The good ones liked the humans and felt sorry for their fragile frames and the meagre time they will spend on the planet. So, out of compassion and empathy they would help these weak mortal beings, keeping them from danger. From time to time they would meet in each other's dwelling, be it a house, cave or ice palace and discuss the deeds they had done. These meetings became more and more frequent and soon they were meeting on a weekly basis, they started to call themselves the marvellous because of the great deeds they did and the fantastic abilities they possessed.

The most serious and unbreakable rule was that the marvellous knew that their powers and ability's must be kept secret. They knew they would be subject to hideous experiments or destroyed in the most hideous ways, for the humans of this world were still barbaric and cruel and they would not care that they had been looked after for hundreds of years by the marvellous. So, as the years trickled by and the marvellous grew strong, they kept the earth safe, they kept their identities and abilities secret and the unruly of themselves at bay, but one night in the years around the early eighteen hundred's superman spotted a strange device. The humans were getting smarter, more intelligent inventions and technology were popping up every day and so a meeting was called.

Immortality

Before we carry on with the meeting we should have a quick word on immortality. The marvellous and the bad super beings are immortal but also slightly A mortal, but only from the things in life that send us humans to the grave. They are immortal to all diseases and viruses, and most of them when cut or wounded (if they can be) will heal very quickly if not immediately, and if they fall from a great height their bones will break, but just like the flesh they will heal fast, but alas they can still die or be killed like any mortal being. We think of vampires as immortal but we know they can still be killed. The A mortal part is that most of them would be dead instantly from a chopped off head, or crushed, or burnt, so the marvellous are well aware of their own mortality when they all come to together to discuss their future.

North Pole 1840 Superman's Crystal Palace

Are story, beginning many years ago, one hundred and twenty to be exact at the home of superman. You know that place he built with that crystal thing. There is serious debate to be had. The humans have invented something called a camera, as superman calls it. It's a not so small device, (in fact it's massive) that records a moment in time. The marvellous know that this is going to be a huge spanner in the works. How can the marvellous go on undetected saving humanity and the world from certain doom every day with stupid humans taking pictures of them? The time has come for a serious debate. Top of the table and leading the talks is superman, next to him his good friend Mr. Fantastic, next to him the Hulk in human form. Others in the room are Mystique, Wolverine, Blade the vampire, Emma frost the ice queen, the Invisible man, Storm, the Sandman and last on the table is Wonder woman, Superman starts the talks. "Marvellous, thank you all for coming. A new menace has been placed in our way, what are we to do about this new demon they call the camera. I know they are few at the moment but in time every human in the world will own one of these things and they will get smaller and smaller for the human's intelligence is increasing at an alarming rate. We have been lucky that they are big and hard to manoeuvre; the hulk just yesterday was nearly caught by one of these things". The Hulk rudely buts in shouting as he bangs his fist on the table. " I would have ripped it from his hands and smashed him to a pulp had he used this device on me". "That hulk my friend is exactly what we don't want, hulk we are here to save the humans to keep them safe. Only just last week I superman was caught on one of these new cameras that catches moving pictures. I was caught flying, but I caught the human and the footage was destroyed so do not fret". "So, what are we to do?" asks storm, "do we stop protecting the humans" "I am afraid so storm" answers superman, "we must disband and we must flee this continent". The Hulk is furious "FLEE, FLEE, he looks around the whole room taking in every eye, I FLEE NO MAN" ... His fists smash to the table and the familiar green sets to his eyes. "Hulk calm down calm down my friend, I am not saying we are to run from humans, we could crush them like grapes, all of us know this, no I am saying let us leave them to their own devices let them kill each other and keep each other in misery", "but Superman what do you mean by flee, it is a strong word" asks Mr. Fantastic. "Yes, yes, sorry I did not mean flee I should have said let us disappear, let us blend into society become like the humans are and do as they do. We should leave this place we call home. We should separate from each other, we should find nice quiet places to live in this vast and beautiful world for it is humongous, and we must forget we are the marvellous". "We all have plenty of the earth currency they call money, we are all immortal, we have possessions now that will be worth much more in the future, keep these things safe and we will live long prosperous lives". The invisible man is in deep thought and superman notices this, you have something on your mind invisible man asks superman? "Yes, I do, what of the evil ones of us, the ones we have been protecting the humans from, will they not be caught by these cameras", "yes they probably will, but their fate is up to themselves, we should only be concerned with our future and where we will go, and that brings me to the worst part of what I must ask you". "We must not tell each other where we are to go, you must leave here now, go out on a journey and find a new home for yourself, you must take on a new identity, become a new person, go now search the globe and find fantastic places to settle. "

As the meeting came to a close superman calls Mr. Fantastic to one side for more serious debate. "We have become good friends you and I yes". "Yes" says Mr. Fantastic. "There is just one thing that bothers me about the tasks we now take. It gives me great pains to ask this favour of you", Mr. fantastic is shocked, he has never seen his friend this vexed. "What is it superman tell me my friend" superman's eyes are on the floor as he rubs his temples, "It is the hulk my friend, he is not very bright and he has tangents, you know this, you are close to the hulk yes", "yes we have been working together for some years now but I am not sure that I could live with him… he is very testing". "Please Mr. fantastic he will not cope in the world out there, he has no patience for the humans, he will turn green, and if he turns green that will be the end of it. You know it takes all of us just to hold him down; he is not in control of his powers". Mr fantastic interrupts angrily, "you do not say these things when he is green and fighting for us, when this happens nobody can stop him not even you superman, yet he always calms down and he always comes back to us". Superman's eyes are still on the floor, he feels shame, "yes I am sorry, I know this, he is invaluable to us, I care for him to and I did not mean to insult him, I am scared for him, out of us all he is the vulnerable one". Mr fantastic smiles at his old friend, "you are correct, I see your point superman, I will do as you wish, you are a good friend", Mr. Fantastic changes the subject. "So, superman where will you go once we disband". Mr fantastic looks to the ceiling shaking his head, "DAM I am sorry superman I have already forgot it is to be a secret". Superman is laughing as he pat's Mr. Fantastic on the back, "It is OK my friend, I will stay here in my crystal palace. I have many crystals to read, things my mother and father wanted me to know. And you Mr. fantastic do you have a place in mind for you and the hulk". "I have not thought about it yet, but we shall probably go somewhere quiet and peaceful that is what I would like I think". "Good, good, I wish you well my friend and may the years be good to you".

So, the marvellous gather together and shake hands and hug for the last time all setting of on new adventures and all promising never to see each other again, or tell each other where they are going, and never use their powers in public. Not unless they are called to do so. Superman steps forward for the last time, "I will find you and call on you all if you are needed but for now go and live your lives in peace".

Liverpool 2009 somewhere overlooking the docks

The Hulk who has now named himself H is running from his bedroom. He still looks exactly the same as he did one hundred and twenty years ago. Tight black curly hair, big blue eyes, quite a handsome face and even though he is in human form he still has the body of a Greek god, his muscles rippling on his six-foot frame. He has risen late, he'd set his alarm clock early so he could go surfing in devil's mouth. (On the subject of the hulk and surfing, the Hulk loves every extreme sport there is, he has a surf board, snow board, skate board, long board skate board, wake board, and he's even tried the new kite surfing and kite beach boarding though I wouldn't say he was any good at them but at least he tries.) As sometimes happens with the technology of today his alarm hasn't gone off, and to be honest He hasn't got up that late, but he's still fuming. "Fuck, fuck, fuck", he says as he runs down the hall, then WHAM, he trips over something and he's flat on his face, at the same time as the Hulk falls a guttural scream of pain comes from the living room, that would be Mr. Fantastic who has named himself Dave, Mr. fantastic still looks the same, straight mousy coloured hair, a very strong Roman looking face, although it is contorted with pain, bright brown eyes, and although not as cut in the muscular department as the hulk he still has a good body on his six-foot three frame. the only thing that's changed allot about Mr. fantastic is that he's one lazy, pot smoking, PlayStation-playing-couch-potato-bastard The Hulk looks down to see what tripped him and sees Dave's cock going into the bathroom, he storms to the living room his eyes green as always when he is furious, "you fucking lazy bastard are you having a fuckin laugh, why can't you just walk to the bog like everyone else, its fuckin disgusting that, ye fuckin cock all over the fuckin house". Dave puts his arms up in a mock surrender, "alright kid take it easy what's got your gripe", "I'm fuckin going surfin and am late, fuckin takes two and a half hours to get there". H is wearing his usual Hulk underpants and storms back to the toilet as Dave's cock slithers back in to his pants. Dave shouts through, "don't know what you're bothered about anyway you've been loads of times and you'll be there all day". H shouts back his temper now receding, "I know but I fuckin love surfing and I fuckin hate getting up late messes with me karma kid, and I hope you haven't been getting stoned and playing that PlayStation all night again, fuckin game junky, do you know how much your addicted to that, you can't even be arsed walking to the fuckin toilet", Dave shouts back in his usual sarcastic tone, "no kid I haven't been on the PlayStation all night, I've been on the Wii, cursed mountain I'm playing, can't get past this fuckin ghost though". The Hulk or H is in the toilet shaking his head and laughing to himself, H has calmed down over the years, he doesn't change anymore, he hasn't for years and that's on account of Dave, his best mucka in the whole world, for one hundred and twenty years they've been partying and bonding, having a laugh, getting pissed, getting stoned, and doing just about every fun thing you could do. Just then there's a knock at the door. And then another, and then another, H shouts from the toilet, "are you going to get that". Then another knock, "fuckin lazy twat ", shouts H, Then another knock. H comes storming out of the bathroom to answer the door and spots Dave's arm stretched all the way from the couch to the door. "Don't you fuckin dare ye bendy bastard" says H as he slaps Dave's hand away; "I'll fuckin tie you in knots". Dave's lying on the couch with the Wii controller in his other hand pissing himself laughing at Hulk, his arm slithers back to normal. The Hulk opens the front door to the surprise and disgust of the postman, seeing the Hulk in his Hulk y fronts. "You have to sign for this mate". "No problemo mucka" says the hulk with not a hint of a Spanish accent. Hulk signs Dave's name and slams the door on the postman. He's holding a letter, its hand written. "What's that" says Dave. "Don't know yet I haven't fuckin opened it have I". He opens the letter and takes out a key card for a door, then starts to read, and as he looks over at Dave he suddenly turns the colour of boiled shite.

Edinburgh Scotland 2009 somewhere overlooking the castle

Mystique who has now named herself Lysa is stretched out on the couch (although Lysa can take on any form she pleases her natural body is not like the one in the movies it's actually fit as fuck, size eight, fantastic ass, beautiful flowing jet-black hair and dazzling bright green eyes she also has a gorgeous little pair of pert breasts that would make any girl green with envy) she's on the phone to a friend. "Yes, I picked him up, I, Yates's wine bar, I was fuckin pissed, but I fuckin remember it alright had a cock on him like a baby's arm. I, that's right all fuckin night. Anyway, got to go he just woke up". Just then a Greek god looking Adonis comes out of the bedroom with just his towel on, Lysa looks him over and says, "you've got muscles on top of your muscles so you have you fuckin hunky bastard "(Lysa fuckin loves sex, and I mean she fuckin LOVES sex, and why shouldn't she, she's fit as fuck, single, got plenty of dosh, and an apartment that would make bill gates say holy shit, but her only downfall is that she loves big cocks, and I mean BIG cocks, not that it's a problem really but sometimes it's just so hard to find a big cock, to be fair, little or average cocks are OK, you know the saying, it's not the size of the boat but the motion of the ocean, but it's no good having great motion if she can't fuckin feel anything, now she can always get the rabbit out if she hasn't been satisfied but she just loves the feel of a big hairy, muscular, sweaty bastard male body on top of her and that's why she's well fuckin pleased with the Adonis, she doesn't even know the cunts name and that makes it all the more fun) "Can I make myself some coffee darling" asks the Adonis, "I, help yourself you wee sexy bastard" she says. Lysa just lays there watching the stud that she fucked all night make coffee, she can still feel the fuckers cock it was that big, like when you've had a tight baseball cap on and when you take it off you can still feel it. "Have you got to go soon or do you fancy a bit of round two". The Adonis looks over to see the absolutely fit as fuck frame of mystique, she's laying just in her sloggy's and belly top, he's thinking of the blow job she gave him before he fucked her last night, he walks over and drops his towel. "Go on then babe get your fuckin lips round that again", "you've got more suck power than a fuckin Henry Hoover" he thinks to himself. Lysa gently lifts the log of meat hanging between his legs and just as she's about to attempt the impossible there's a knock at the door. "What a twat, there's always a knock when you're in the middle of something, who the fucks knocking this early" says Lysa as she drops the cock and trots to the door in her sloggy's. She opens the door to the surprise and delight of the postman; well it was delight until he looks further in the room and sees the Adonis, a huge slab of muscle and a fuckin baby's arm dangling. "You have to sign for this love". "I right". She says before slamming the door in the postman's face. As she rips the hand-written envelope open she's thinking of what she will do to the Adonis as she trots back and plants herself down, but as she opens the letter a key card falls on to her lap she starts to read the letter and the Adonis watches her suddenly turn the colour of boiled shite.

London 2009 somewhere overlooking the docks

The invisible man, who has named himself Sid is looking at his stalking pictures. Unlike the others and true to his old self, the invisible man is skinny, has greasy black hair, and most of the time fuckin stinks, he has a really bad hygiene problem and only gets a shower when he knows the women might smell him, he's only small about four foot two, and has a ugly pointy jagged face, and his eyes don't look like they have any colour at all, they just look like small black points) "yes, yes, yes", this is a good one he thinks, he's looking at one of his new victims, she is fit as fuck, blond, big tits, her ass sticks out that much you could hold your pint on it. Sid has always been a pervert but as technology grew so did his obsession. He has his system down to a tee now, he spots a bird he likes follows her home, invisible of Course, he usually watches her for a bit, watches' her undress, he likes to get risky and walk right up to them and have a little sniff, see what perfume she's wearing, then usually he stands in the corner and has a wank, and if he's lucky her fella might be home and he gets a full show, well now and then he gets a full show, it's amazing how little married folks fuck. Now, the girls who are married or with boyfriends are crap really because that's all he can do, have a wank and watch her boyfriend fuck her so no, fuck them married ones, he likes the single ones more, then he can put his full plan into action. He stalks' them for a few weeks, sits in their flat or house and watches them for hours, it's great when a girl doesn't know she's being watched, the fuckin positions they get into when their shaving their fanny's and doing their exercises. He'll take some photos and video for his private collection. (Remember whatever the invisible man is holding is invisible also, so although he hasn't tried it he could come in with an entire film crew if they all held hands, but alas, its usually just him and his camera's.) So, when he's finished or bored with the photos he gets himself fully worked up and he goes for it. He waits until she goes to sleep, gives her a little chloroform just enough to keep her out, sets up his video cameras and he's away, the dirty bastards fuck's every hole the poor girls got. When he's finished he gets himself some fem fresh and gives her a good clean up, tidy's the room and jobs a good'n, then he's off, he usually goes home to watch his new movie and crack one off. So, as he's looking at the pictures of his new victim and thinking of the night of pure pleasure to come, there's a knock at the door, he stashes his stuff and opens the door to the postman, "special delivery mate you have to sign for it". The invisible man signs his name slams the door in the postman's face, he rips his letter open and a key card hits the floor, he glances at the note that came with the key card, it's at this moment he decides to turn the colour of boiled shite.

Birmingham 2009 The City Centre

Blade who has now called himself Brian, is about to make a shit load of money, not that he needs it. After 120 years of collecting shite, you know brick-a-brack-shity antiques and such he doesn't need money. In fact, all of the marvellous share this common trait, they're all fuckin minted, and each have their own little money-making schemes. It takes away the boredom of the years. (blade is a six foot three extremely handsome black man, with smouldering deep brown eyes, very much like his comic book, movie persona, in fact blade styles himself exactly on himself, he wears long black leather matrix coat, has the Chelsea seven stripe going through his short fro, and can walk in the daylight, unlike the movie blade he doesn't know if other vampires can walk in the day because he's never met one. But he does have to drink blood human blood, but luckily for him not that much nowadays, and also unlike the movie blade he doesn't give a fuck, he just finds a wino or a smack head or just a piece of shit human and drinks the life from them. Also unlike the comic book blade he has no idea how old he is or when he was made a vampire, he just knows it wasn't in the way the movie makes out, he was definitely only a teenager when he was made because he still only looks about nineteen) So blade has got himself into free running he fuckin loves it, but then it is pretty easy for a vampire, he can scale walls and jump buildings better than that Spiderman-cunt-fuckin-web-shooting-faggot, I never liked that cunt, mumbling bastard, I'd take that fucker on any day he thinks to himself. So, Blade was ready to take on the brummy crew, a nice gang of lads and girls to be honest, they'd been free running for years now and held a competition every Saturday night so as to keep up their skills, and Brian or Blade to us was the man to beat. There were ten runners in the line-up all hoping and jumping with excitement, some were doing back flips to show off their skills, the runners know the race is soon to start when a slow base line rumble starts up, it's the massive attack song Angel, no one can see were the music is coming from but a few of the runners have got sly smiles on their faces as the base line rumbles BUM DE DUM DE DUM BUM. Then a sexy little bird walks out in front of the runners, just like in an American collage race queen, she has two handkerchiefs' in her hands lifted high, Blade was clocking her ass, "she's fit as fuck" he was thinking, he'd wanted to fuck her for ages but she was going with one of the other runners, he was so mesmerised by the glorious globe of an ass that he missed the start, before he knew anything her hands were by her sides and everyone was off. Not that it mattered to Blade within seconds he was with them scooting up walls. Two quick steps, a massive leap to the drain pipe and a flip over the parapet and he was off. The whole crew looked up to blade like he was a god and he was to them, he could jump higher and further and run faster, so as usual at the end of the race Blade was taking the money. He wasn't a cunt though he'd often go out with his money buying new equipment and clothes for the crew which made him even more likeable, he fuckin loved the kids and that's why he hung around with them, even though he was centuries old, he fuckin hated old miserable cunts all they do is fuckin moan and groan, no, give me the young ones any day, they were everything to him all they did was have fun, and he was terrified for the day that would come soon when they'd have to grow up and become the cunts he hated. he pondered these thoughts as he raced over the roofs of Birmingham on his way home, it was early morning and as he swung into his apartment "he always left the window open because no cunt would ever be able to reach it but him" he heard the bell go, when he answered the door there was a postman with a letter, "you have to sign for this mate", Blade signs the form and rips the hand written letter open, he takes out the key card and reads the letter that comes with it, then he turns the colour of boiled shite.

Wales Cardiff 2009 somewhere overlooking the sea

Storm who has now called herself Mel has just got back from a fuckin bang top rave. Cardiff is fuckin rocking these days and Wales itself is one of the best rave up places in England, and she should know, she's been to them all, the academy, cream, the state, escape, legends, garlands, the edge, the quadrant park, ministry of sound, fantasia, the hacienda, it's even better than Ibiza or Ayia Napa sometimes, but you know let's not take the piss I did say sometimes. Yes, Storm was a raver and a fuckin top one at that, the only time she used her powers is if the weather was shity at the rave, other than that the girl was just after a good time. Like mystique, Mel is fit as fuck, tall, six foot, she looked like skin from Skunk Anansie except she never had a bald bonce, she had a fit little tight fro, and if she was standing in front of you naked she would look like a piece of chiselled marble, that's how toned her body was, she had gorgeous big brown eyes, and a massive pair of tits. She wasn't overly sexually motivated but she did love a good fuck every now and again, but her main passion was drugs, she fuckin loved drugs, and she poured as many down her throat as humanly possible, not that she was human, but you know, figure of fuckin speech. The great thing about not being human was that although the drugs gave her the same affects as it did humans, she'd feel the rush of the tablet, then the steady eddy, then the rushes again, but it did fuck all to her body, her mind and immune system, she could switch off from the effects any time she chose, she was living the fuckin life. So Storm has just got in, she was at a pretty good rave tonight but she misses the old raves and the old players, she was there when it all kicked off in eighty seven, the second summer of love they called it, and the tablets will never be as good, them doves were the best thing she's ever had, she sometimes wishes she saved a few, you know put some away for a rainy day, but who was to know that twenty odd years later they'd be shit, back then you only had to take one and you'd be off your Barnet all night, you'd have to take ten now to get that kind of a buzz. And the fuckin DJ's were the best Stu Allen, Groovrider, The Rat Pack, Slip-mat, Carl Cox and the king of the rave the one and only TOP BUZZ, he was a fuckin genus, she remembers being at a fantasia in an old abandoned air craft carrier in Exeter and when top buzz came on she nearly pissed herself the crowd went fuckin ballistic, but c'est la fuckin vie time ticks on she's thinking and David Guetta's quite good to be honest. she hasn't brought a man home tonight because she couldn't be arsed with the conversation, she's feeling that beautiful next-day-no-sleep-early morning hazy feeling of the speed (the tablets have well-worn off) she's knocked herself a couple of big fat joints, amnesia haze and blue cheese, she's got her rabbit out because there's no better feeling than toking on a joint while the rabbit dose the biz on her man in the boat, she's just about to spark the joint and drop her knickers when there's a knock at the door, she opens it to the postman who gets a right semi on when he sees her standing in her sloggy's with rabbit in hand, her fuckin thud is that fat she looks like she's got a cock, and her sloggy's are stretched that tight across her pussy he can see her sweet-ass pubes and camel toe. (yes, that's how closely he looks) he's fuckin trembling as he asks "can you sign for this love", the postman has about twenty seconds of fantasy flashing through his brain before he is presented with the door slamming in his face. Although storm is pale and pasty and looking rather fucked from all the drugs she had the night before, when she opens the hand-written letter she still turns the colour of boiled shite,

Newcastle 2009 somewhere by the docks

Wolverine who has now called himself Brian, is one boring bastard to tell the truth, he still looks fantastic as do all the marvellous (again he is six one dark wavy hair as depicted in the comic books and movies, even though, like Blade, he is a bit vain and styles himself on his comic book or movie self, he has the massive sideburns and a fantastic physique, brown eyes massive hands and a pretty handsome face to boot) but over the years he has become bored with life. After being alive for god knows how long he's fed up. He thinks he's done it all, and now he sits there contemplating his life, well, his past sixty years or so to be honest. He's been a teddy boy, rockabilly, hippy, mod, rocker, punk, skinhead, new wave romantic, raver, heavy metal head, Mosher, Goth, and any other stereotype you could think of. He's also listened and bought every one of these musical genres so you can imagine the size of the cunts record collection, and his wardrobe. He's done every fighting method known to man, he's done wrestling, boxing, cage fighting, kung foo, karate, kick boxing, thi bo, thi boxing, judo, jujitsu, Ikedo, you name it he's done it, he's even done that crazy Brazilian dancing fighting thing capoeira (not that he's a bully or a hard case, he's actually quite nice and mild mannered, he just wanted to keep up with the persona) But lately he's just been bored, I suppose we all get like that and I suppose after one hundred and twenty years without seeing his friends he should be bored. He's even considered killing himself but it's so fucking hard when your immortal. He sits on his beautiful couch in his massive apartment springing his blades in and out of his hands. he's thinking about the marvellous and the fact that he hasn't seen them for over a hundred years. He wonders where in the world they are and what they're doing now. He hasn't thought about his old friend in years and wonders what has brought on this new bout of melancholy. I wonder how Mr. Fantastic and the Hulk are doing. The Hulk was always so unpredictable and Mr. Fantastic always so sensible. He thinks of mystique and the other girls, they were all fit as fuck, he wonders if any of them married, probably not, it was so hard being what they were and never ageing. There was never any problem with the sex, they were all the same as humans in that department, you just had to be a bit gentler or you could rip the poor girl in half. He remembers once just as he was shooting his load, his blades also shooting out of his knuckles, luckily for the girl and himself his fists were on the mattress. She asked him what had happened later and he just said he ripped the mattress in a state of ecstasy, which is pretty much the truth. So, with wolverine feeling miserable and lonely, when the postman knocks on his door and asks him to sign for his letter, rather than turning the colour of boiled shite, he's absolutely ecstatic and as he pockets his key card he screams yeeeeeeee haaaaaarr, it's about time mother fuckers.

Newquay 2009 Watergate bay overlooking the sea

The sandman who has called himself Brodi (sad bastard was brad before he saw Point Break) sits on the balcony of his shit hot apartment watching the waves crashing to the shore. He's purchased apartments all over the world and all of them are beach front. This definitely has something to do with the fact that he is always shedding sand and likes to replenish himself, unlike the others the sandman finds it easy to move around the world on the account that he obviously can turn to sand, he just goes where the cold wind blows. The sandman is a big fucker, not tall really, about five feet seven, but he looks like the cage fighter chuck Liddell, wider than he is tall. (the daft cunt even thought of calling himself the ice man if he ever became a superhero again until he remembered that he was made of sand, fuckin bell end) his best features are his striking green eyes, and he's got fuckin massive mitts, he's not that good looking though, now this isn't to say that chuck Liddell isn't good looking just in case I ever meet the cunt, but he looks like one of them Planet of the Apes dolls you got when you were young, you know the ones where you put your fingers in the back and squished up the face, o and he fuckin loves the ocean, that's the other reason for all the beach front properties, and if the Hulk knew what I am about to tell you next he would definitely turn green, not with anger, but with pure jealousy, the sandman is one of the best unknown surfers in the world, he can surf a wave like john Holmes could fuck a woman. (this also probably has something to do with the fact that the cunt has lived on the beach for a hundred and twenty years) the sandman loves Cornwall and comes back every summer, it's one of the most relaxing places in the world, and since most of the hot places in the world have their summer in the winter, it suits him to a tee, he's just got back from his other beach house in morocco, and as I said he's sitting on his balcony overlooking the sea, he's got a Remy martin and coke on the table and a nice fat Moroccan joint in the ashtray, the sun is cracking the flags, Radiohead are playing on his boss iPod docking station, could life get any better, Thom Yorke is singing how to disappear completely and a joint ready to be sparked. The sandman picks up his joint and takes a huge toke, the song and the weed make him feel like he's floating on a bed of silk, a bit fuckin deep but Radiohead always make him feel like that, he's looking at his mail which is also on the table, a fuckin big stack which he hasn't read for months, he fights off the pot daemon in his head that's saying just fuckin leave it and starts to flick through it when he comes across a hand written letter, which the cleaner has signed for, strange he thinks what the fucks this, he opens the letter, wonders what the key card's for, then starts to read. Now because he's made of sand I can't really say he turns the colour of boiled shite but that's definitely what happens.

London 2009 somewhere in Chelsea

Emma frost who has kept the name Emma has just got back from a shopping trip in L.A. she's sitting in one of the plushest apartments in Chelsea, and she's drooling over her new jimmy chews, she bought six pairs, and a shit load of other stuff, (to the delight of the custom official, "you've got to pay duty on them love") but she didn't mind she fuckin well minted. (Out of all the girls we have talked about up until now Emma is definitely the bimbo of the crowd. not that she's a fuckin thick as fuck blond, because she actually very intelligent. But she is blond, and I am talking Pam Anderson blond, and while we're on the subject of Pamela Anderson they might as well be twins, because that's what she looks like, fit as a butcher's fuckin dog, as I said blond hair right down her back, gorgeous big brown eyes, a little five-foot four frame. An ass that would make the pope cry, ten-inch waist, and let's not even talk about her Pammy's, she is most definitely the stereotypical Californian beach babe) She's wondering which jimmy's to wear tonight when she meets the girls, she hasn't seen them for a while and she wants, no loves, to see them squirm with jealousy. Not that she hates or dislikes her girlfriends she just loves being a bitch. She pops her iPod into her fatman docking station and flicks to the freemasons, these are fuckin great to listen to while you're getting ready to go out, she turns the two-thousand-pound valve system up so she can feel the base on the floor as the freemasons scream out when you touch me, and then she's bopping round the apartment thinking to herself fuck the neighbours. She goes into her walk-in closet (or I should say full fuckin size dressing room to tell the truth) and looks at the four dresses she's picked out, there's a Balmain, Kaufman Franco, Azzaro, and a really sexy David Koma, she's pondering on how to mix and match but then decides, who gives a fuck, they all cost so much no one will give a fuck, she decides on the Kaufman Franco because it was the most expensive, she's going to look amazing. She then picks out a gorgeous little Di Murini lingerie set; she hangs the full outfit up with the Jimmy Chews to see how they will look. Shit fucking hot is what she's thinking. There's absolutely no fuckin chance she's bringing a man home tonight, that Kaufman Franco is not getting turned into a Monica Lewinski. She strips off to get in the shower and notices that her beaver is getting a little overgrown and decides it's not fair on the little Di Murini number to be subjected to that, so it's out with the epilator and off with the bush. She's sitting on the floor legs akimbo looking at her snatch and wondering if she should go for an all-out Kojak, she decides on a landing strip to save time and pain, not that she feels much pain but when you go Kojak you do get quite close to the man in the boat, and when your rushing you could just clip it and she just hasn't got the time to be careful. Like the sandman Emma has been out of town for a while and once she's done the three S's you know shit, shave, shower, she makes herself a Kopi Luwak coffee, you know the expensive one that's made from cat shit, (because I think you've gathered by now that with Emma it's all about the expense, if it doesn't cost the earth I don't fuckin want it) so while she's drinking her cat shit coffee she rolls herself a joint of yes you guessed it the most expensive weed you can get. (it's not really the best weed actually it's just plain old crap English home grown skunk but that's what the dealer blagged her with, probably good for her to be honest because if it was proper Amsterdam skunk she wouldn't be going out tonight shed be on her fuckin back snoring like a cunt) she's flicking through her mail and there's plenty of it (fuckin junk mail) when she sees a hand written letter that the maid had signed for, she opens it puts the key card on the table and starts to read. What a shame, all that work on her pussy and getting her clothes ready when after all she won't be going out tonight. And even though the skunks shit she does go a bit faint and yes, she does turn the colour of boiled shite.

The Manor 2009

Spiderman is in the manor house making sure all the cameras and sound are in place, the manor has been fitted out with plasmas, all the latest home cinema surround sound, huge leather sofas, lap tops, full sky HD TV, the fucking lot. Spiderman is scuttling across the ceiling fitting the cameras, he's got his lap top plugged into the sound system, there's a Cure song playing from his laptop, it's that creepy song they did called lullaby and it fits to the scene perfectly, because Spiderman has got a gross way of climbing around, kind of creepy with a weird little stutter and this weird little stutter fits in time to the music, he's singing to the song in his mumbled voice, he has a hand held monitor to watch as he puts his cameras in place, they're so tiny no one could see them and with all the chandeliers in this place the jobs a good'n, he's got fifty cameras and fifty audio devices to fit, and then set the Wi-Fi hub up on the roof, then its home James.

The Letter

Dear the marvellous, I bet it's a long time since you've heard that name, because it's a very long time since I have used it, I shall keep this letter short and sweet, you have all been invited to spend a month at my manor house, it has been way over a century since our remarkable paths last crossed, so now is the time I think, for us to become reacquainted with each other, do not fret about the time I have asked you to spend, bring whatever belongings you need there is plenty of room for all.

North pole 2009 Superman's Crystal Palace

Superman sits alone in his crystal palace as he has done for the past one hundred and twenty years. He would have liked to have kept his promise of watching over the marvellous which he did for some time, but then when everyone had settled in their new lives and he watched them become more and more normal he thought it better to leave them to their own devises. Maybe in hindsight it was a bad idea because superman is fuckin loop de loop, and wouldn't you be after one hundred and twenty years alone, (well nearly one hundred and twenty, apart from a one-time excursion to which he has never recovered mentally, and always regretted, it's his biggest secret, and if the others knew what he had done he's one hundred percent certain that there would be fuckin murders. Superman won't receive a letter because the letter sender doesn't not know where the fuck he lives, and it would be quite hard and an unbelievable fucking achievement for a postman to deliver a letter to the furthest corner of the North Pole, not that the north pole has corners, and a secret crystal palace to boot. So, as I said earlier superman sits alone pondering the strange feeling he has in his gut, he had the weirdest feeling that his beloved marvellous are in danger, he doesn't know where this feeling comes from, or why he feels it at this very moment he just knows he's never felt it before, I must ask the crystals he shouts, to absolutely nobody. (Before we carry on let's get ourselves up to speed with the crystals, as you know when superman was a super teenager he went to the North Pole and threw the green crystal which made the palace. Once he got to the palace there was a row of crystals, sent from his mother and father with information about who he was and where he came from, and a brief description of what type of person he may become on planet earth, now the crystals were a kind of hologram, with just a small part of his parents intelligence and mind body and spirit mixed in, they weren't really real and only had limited knowledge, so as you can imagine after one hundred and twenty years of listening to superman and answering his questions they were bored as shit and fucking hated his guts, even though they were just holograms they had taken on a life of their own, probably due to the fact that superman bought them a TV., he even hooked a satellite up, he said it was so they could watch the progression of the human race.) superman runs into the crystal room, "mother, father, we must have serious debate, I have the strangest feeling in my stomach and I fear for the marvellous", the faces of superman's mother and father appear, "yes my son the feeling in your stomach is probably the condition the humans call the shits, ha, ha," the hologram of superman's dad is laughing its ass off, that is, if a hologram had an ass, Lara, superman's mum cuts in "Jor-el, be quiet our son is in need of our assistance", the hologram of Jor-el looks puzzled and turns to his wife who gives him the stone face look, which all men alien or human know as shut your fuckin mouth, Lara, out of the side of her mouth whispers "I will tell you later, just go with it, yes son, I too have had this strange feeling and if I were you I would be terrified for your friends". Jor-el at last gets wise to his wife's plan, fuck me he's thinking, for a hologram she is fuckin shit hot, he decides to play along, "yes son I too fear for your friends, we feel they are in great peril". Jor-el pauses for maximum effect, he knows his dippy ass son loves the dramatics. "We feel a new evil has arisen, you must go to them". Lara looks to her husband with her eyebrows raising in approval and a fuckin big smile on her face, "yes son listen to your father he knows best". "But mother father I cannot leave this palace it is too dangerous; do you not remember what happened the last time I ventured out". "You dwell on the past to harshly son, accidents can and will happen, but you must put the past behind you, your friends are the most important thing at this very moment". "Yes, yes, as always you are correct I will ponder your thoughts before I decide, thank you mother and father, as always you are my guiding light". Superman walks away feeling a bit confused, his mother and father were quite nice to him tonight and that was unusual, they usually shouted obscenities at him like, wanker, no hoper, useless cunt, retard, and quite often reminded him that he was shit scared to go outside, they laughed, ha, ha, the son of Jor-el a super being was scared to face the nasty humans. But they are right thought superman, why am I scared to leave this palace? have I caught some crazy human virus? I have much to ponder, yes much to ponder.

Jor-el and Lara watch superman walk out of the crystal room, then they turn to each other with big cheesy grins. "Do you think he will go", asks Lara, "yes he will go, he is too scared for the wellbeing of his friends, at last a bit of peace from the boring bastard", "o yes I am delighted, only one nights grace in over a hundred years, I will dance the jig the night he goes", "but Jor-el, how long do you think it will be? he never leaves, I think he has the human condition agoraphobia" Jor-el ponders this for a while and then gives his wife a sly look as he answers, "then we will have to push him more, we will leave him for a while he is probably suspicious, we haven't been this nice to him for years, let his mind dwell on his friends and then when he is really fretting for them, we will push".

The Cave 2009

Spiderman scuttles across the wall of the cave where he lives, he is on his way back to see his master, and he just needs a quick detour to his room. Spiderman is one of those superheroes that Stan got a bit wrong, he's not really a superhero but more a super villain, he's always been bad if he thinks about it, he just gets mad at his condition most of the time, see, it's not a suit that Spiderman wears, the suit is his actual skin, that's the real him, there is no fucking suit and how weird is that. So, let's have a look at his anatomy, he has no toes, just them weird round stumpy feet things (but they do stick well to walls) weird webbed fingers (these also stick well to walls) he's blue and red, has big massive black eyes and has no mouth, he sounds like Kenny from Southpark when he talks which makes people laugh at him, not that he socialises much which is probably why he's a villain, but the weirdest part of Spiderman's anatomy as you have seen but probably never realised is that he has no cock, yes that's right he has no fucking cock, just a patch, he doesn't miss a cock though because he's never had one and what you've never had you'll never miss, but this also is a huge laughing matter for anyone he meets, so he fucking hates humans, the dirty weak bastards, and he's been waiting years for the chance to wipe the fuckers out. Just let them fagot marvellous cunts try and stop us; the boss has got something wicked in store for you cunts. Spiderman creeps into his room, the room is fabulous and its fuckin massive, fifty inch plasma hi def, surround sound, PlayStation 3, Wii, Xbox and the biggest loudest Bang and Olufsen sound system you've ever seen, they all line one wall with a wraparound couch, on another wall there's thousands of CD's DVDs and games (but no porno's because he hasn't got a cock) also in his room there's a mini gym in the corner with bags and a kung foo training horse, there's a massive computer terminal with multiscreen like in the movie Hackers (he copied it actually) where he does his surfing and other stuff for the boss, the walls are adorned with posters of his favourite bands and idols, the stooges, Jimi Hendrix, the Beatles, the who, Bruce lee, Ian Curtis, Curt Cobain, etc, (but no sexy models because he hasn't got a cock) he's also done some very good drawings across the walls, there's lots from the movie pink Floyd the wall (the teacher, the hammers, and the ass judge) and a massive Jim Morrison head like in the Lost Boys. (He copied that as well) but as I said earlier no women though because he's got no cock. He's just bought a new processor for a pc he's building and he wants to fit it before he goes to the boss. He's a computer genus now, mostly because he's a recluse, he stayed in for years and became a wonder on the old pc, mostly because he wasn't surfin for porn, and that's why the boss loves him, he's the bosses numero Uno, or so he thinks, when he's done he scuttles across the ceiling to the main room where he knows the boss will be. "Hello Spidey" shouts the boss when he sees him "my faithful friend return's as always, not like her" the boss mutters to himself "she's been gone far too long, far too long" Magneto opens his arms to the ceiling "come in, and how did it go my wonder webbed friend, did everything go to plan"? Spiderman slides down his web and lands next to the boss and answers in his muffled tongue, "yes boss everything is in order, the mansion is ready for them, all the cameras are in place, they are state of the art high definition, we won't miss a thing, and the audio is sublime, I have fitted them all over, even in the gardens". "And what of the letters, asks the boss, have they been sent out"? "Yes, I made sure of it myself since you cannot trust this buffoon". Spiderman jabs a finger at Sabretooth who is also in the room but has been very quiet until now, he roars at Spiderman, "I will rip your fuckin head off, fuckin no dick", he grabs Spiderman by the throat and is about to give him a pummelling but the boss comes between them, all Magneto does is give Sabretooth a look and he shrinks like a mistreated dog. "I have told you sabretooth I will not tell you again if you ever touch him I will slice you up with a Stanley blade and cover you in salt, now fuck off back to your corner". Sabretooth is livid and ashamed, he can see Spiderman is smirking and he wants to wipe the smug smile off his face, my time will come he thinks, the boss won't always be here to protect the little cunt, (of all the bad super beings out there you have to feel sorry for Sabretooth, it's not that he's bad its more that he's as thick as two short planks, he's definitely one of the oldest, from right back to prehistoric times, he's immortal but that's about it, he can't do much else, he's just a man mountain and very loyal, which is a shame because if the marvellous were the first to meet him he would probably be a good guy, but unfortunately for him he was recruited by the boss many hundreds of years ago, so this life is the only life the poor bastard knows) Sabretooth slopes off to his room and leaves the boss and Spiderman to their talks, which is mostly of revenge.

Liverpool, 2009

H was thinking about packing the car, well if you can call an Audi Q7 a car, more like an urban assault vehicle. H fuckin loves Audis, he's had them for years, his first was an Audi eighty quarto, he had a few of them until the S4 came out, then the RS4, he's now got an R8 Spider V10 and he fuckin loves it, but it's not very practical for surfing and stuff so he got the Q7, he was going to pack enough gear for a month, but then he thought fuck it, I'm not leaving all me gear here for fuck knows how long, whoever this cunt is who sent the letter, if he wants me to come live in a fuckin manor house he'll have to take me and me gear, I'm getting a removal van and were goin in the R8. The next day the van arrives and its heave fucking ho, the hulk's got tonnes of shite and it's all going in, "I bet all you take is some clothes and your fuckin PlayStation" he says to Dave as he brings more and more boxes from his room, "no kid shouts Dave the Wii's comin as well, and me iPod", H shakes his head laughing and carry's his box down stairs, he doesn't trust the removal men to carry his gear but he didn't know this until they turned up at his door, when they turned up the meet and greet went something like this, four men get out of the van, they're pretty big lads from all the moving they do every day, but that doesn't bother H, the four lads are standing in a line and H is sizing them up, first off three of them are smoking and H doesn't like that, H only smokes joints, he doesn't see the point of smoking ciggys because they don't do fuck all to you, if you're going to smoke he thinks you may as well get something out of it, so the lads are standing in front of H smoking ciggys the way scouse lads do, they kind-of suck on the ciggy like it's the last one they're ever going to smoke, sucking on it so hard that the end looks like a blow torch, they also blow it out like they're trying to blow out a hundred birthday candles or that they've just learned that they give you cancer and they want the smoke out of their lungs as soon as possible, as I said H is giving them the once over and they're doing the same as scouse lads do, and H doesn't like that either, so rather than fuck around H does his usual trick and tells it like it is, "right lads, no offence but I don't like the look of ye, I've got loads of expensive and fragile shit ere, so do us a favour and fuck off for a couple of hours, al give ye a bell when am done an ye can drive it up then". The lads are a little insulted but like good old scouser's they know when their lucks in, rather than argue or take offence they just fuck off the ale house for a couple of hours. Twenty minutes later H is sweating his balls off, he's thinking to himself as he loads the truck, Fuckin hell av got fuckin loads to do yet, a should of let them lazy cunts do this I'm fuckin payin them, but I just know one of the cunts would of banged me surf board, an I'd have had to fuckin bang him, as he's thinking this to himself he's clenching his fist as if the lads have already done it and he's about to land one on them, that's what he's thinking and saying out loud to himself as he loads the van, as well as his surfboard, snowboard and bindings, skateboards, inline skates, wakeboard,(don't know when or where he's going to use them) he's got shit loads of clothes, and all his electrical equipment just in case, you know, projector media player, iPod docking station with video output, laptop, HD video camera, Nintendo ds, and PSP, also he wouldn't be going anywhere without his Rickenbacker 700c Comstock acoustic, its white with a black rim and a sweet gold scratch board, and let's not forget the Gibson doves in flight, that cost him a few bob, when he gets back up to the apartment he's pleasantly surprised to see Dave has got off his ass and done a bit of packing, in fact he's fuckin done loads, he can be very fast and useful when he's not stoned, he's standing in the hall by the front door and his arms are going ten to the dozen in and out of rooms like big elastic bands, each time they come back they have something he wants to take and it goes into the boxes that (to h's astonishment) have been labelled. Dave turns round as his arms come back with the PlayStation and a fuckin massive bong, "that's me done kid, wanna help me load it in the car", H shakes his head, "are you fuckin takin that", he points to the massive bong, "yer kid we might av a bong party, ye never know", H just starts laughing and grabs a few of Dave's boxes, he's in good spirits today, the letter brought back lots of forgotten memories for both of them, so today is going to be a very big day, when H read the letter to Dave that morning they both sat flabbergasted, they spent all day and they stayed up all night trying to recall memories and remember people and names. But they weren't that successful, except for a few comic books with a couple of real tales. see most of the super beings be it good or bad have memories like you and me they remember last week fine and last month, but you don't remember every single moment, and then when you try to remember years gone by you only recall the good moments and they come in a weird dream like haze, and when you've spent the last fifty years getting stoned, as H and Dave have your even more fucked, so if it wasn't for the comic books and movies they'd be really fucked, and that was the dilemma or question they pondered through most of that night. How the fuck did Stan know all the stuff he knew, somebody must have told him, even if it was muddled. And who was the invite from, that was another big question, who owned the manor they were about to live in. The next morning the pair of them are in good spirits as they load the last of Dave's stuff in the van. "The lads will be back in an hour kid an then were off", they both slap each other on the back with big cheesy grins on their faces. An hour later their sitting in the R8 Spider V10, "shall I put the roof down kid" asks H, "yer if you want mucker, give me hair a good blow dry", they're laughing again as H puts the post code into the satnav, "that's us all set ye fuckin crazy contortionist, let's fuckin go".

London the dock's 2009

Sid the invisible man felt strange when he got the letter, it stirred up some strange memories, when he read the word, marvellous, he was shocked to remember he was a good guy, because for years and years he has been a recluse, not really mixing with people, and he also became a stalker and a sex beast, so for a long time when he thinks of what type of person he is and what he does, he comes to the conclusion that he is a bad person. But now this letter has brought back memories of a better past, a past when he was good, he remembered a lot yesterday and last night, and starts to feel good again, anyway he thinks, I'm not that bad cos I only done what every man would do if they could turn invisible, he knows this because he's asked most of them, before he started beasting women he'd ask random men he met in the boozer, what would you do mate if you could turn invisible and whatever your holding turns invisible as well, ninety five percent of the answers are, ide go straight round to so and so's and watch her get her kit off, fuckin darling she is, hold on govna did you say anything am holding is invisible as well, ide probably video it as well so I can crack on off later ha, ha, ha. So, it's no wonder he started doing it really, after so many men saying the same thing, it maybe, just a little, got out of control, o and the other five percent said they'd rob a bank and that's men for you. so Sid starts to buck up and he's looking forward to the trip, he's a bit of a minty bastard so he decides to have a good scrub up before he goes, he's not taking much just clothes for a month, he's got some Armani suits, they fit him well because he's small, and he's got some chill out clothes sweat pants and jumpers and stuff, and he'd never leave without his HD video camera, he's assuming the place will have everything else he needs, he's been trying to remember what the others looked like but he can't, the only reason he remembers them at all is those fuckin comic books, and how the fuck did Stan know all that, even if some of its bullshit and mixed up, he can't wait to ask them that one, and who's the fucking letter off, that's what he wants to know. He tries to remember the girls and what they look like, he's hoping their fit, and then he remembers that crazy cunt Hulk, he hopes he isn't going to be there, he used to scare the shit out of me, he wonders if he's mellowed out. So, with all this on his mind, Sid goes down with his bags to his BMW X6, he got this for his equipment and a fast getaway, he fuckin loves driving this, and it looks fuckin beautiful from the back, he starts the bitch up and listens to the sweet rumble of the twin power turbo v8 engine for a minute, then he punches the post code into the onboard satnav and he's off.

Newcastle 2009

Brian or Wolverine is still chuffed as fuck he hasn't slept a wink all night, it's like he's on speed or coke but he never touches the stuff, he can't believe he's going to meet the gang again, unlike most of the marvellous Brian has been keeping a diary, he saw the comic books when they first came out and wondered how in the hell Stan knew what he knew, even though some of the stories were wrong or twisted it was incredible that Stan still knew so much, so he's been reading his own diary's and trying to remember good stories to tell that he knows the others won't remember, (as I said earlier he's a boring fucker.) he cannot wait to meet the others he's been waiting years for this, as soon as he saw the letter he knew it was from superman, it had to be, but what he's really looking forward to is seeing his old crush mystique, O yes she was beautiful, now nothing ever happened between them , she didn't even know he liked her, but for Brian she was his first love. Brian is packing, just enough clothes for a month, some diesel chill-out clobber, and two Leonard Logsdail suits, and he's definitely taking his beard trimmer, his weights and bench, his kung foo horse, and most of his other martial arts training equipment, and all his training suits, and like Hulk he hired a van to take his gear up to the manor house. Also he knows the others are going to be flashing the style, he just knows it and he wants to be the top mother fucker there, so it's a flip between the silver Aston Martin DBS, an absolute fuckin killer of a car, you don't have to hear the engine you can tell just by looking at the fucker that it's going to be a beast, or should he take his other Aston Martin, a red V8 Vantage roadster, not as powerful and beastly looking as the DBS but beautiful and elegant plus the fuckin top comes off, he can't pick and its frazzling his brain, he just knows if he doesn't go in the convert some other cunt will, but he wants to show the power and brute strength of the DBS, it's a fuckin hard life, he finally decides on the DBS, fuck the convert he's thinking as he throws his bag in the boot, he jumps in, gives his wolverine wobbly head that stands on his dashboard a flick, (and yes he has fucking ruined a Aston Martin DBS by putting a fucking wolverine wobbly head on the dashboard.) then its post code in the satnav and were off.

Newquay 2009

Brodi the Sandman is still on the veranda, he reminisced, got pissed on brandy, and smoked most of his Moroccan then fell asleep, he was woken up by the sun warming his face, what a beautiful feeling, probably one of the greatest feelings you can ever experience, you are asleep and you feel your face cooking, you begin to wake but you don't want to, you wish just for a dreamy second that you could lie there forever feeling that warmth on your face. And that's one of the other reasons he always lives on the beach, he sparks a spliff and thinks about his day to come, he was a bit pissed off because he's only just got back and now he's got to go again, but luck be a lady, it's not that far, he's wearing some Billabong shorts and his Iggy and stooges t shirt and he decides, fuck it, that's all I'm taking shorts and tee's, and one suit, a fine ass Gucci number, so it shouldn't take long to do his packing, in all ten of his beach front apartments he has two or three cars and jeeps, in his Watergate bay apartment he has the Mitsubishi L200 walkinshaw, a beast of a van for sure, and an Audi TT

RS roadster. He decides to go in the Audi, he's not taking that much and if he needs more he can always pop back, as he toke's on his joint he starts to think of the others again, he hasn't thought of them much, except when comic books came out, and then the movies, now that was a shock, how the fuck did Stan Lee know all that, where did he get it all from, he vaguely remembers a vow of silence, somebody must have broken it, he remembers Superman putting it in place and wonders how pissed he must have been when he saw it. That gets him thinking of the invite and who could have sent it, it must be superman it couldn't be anyone else. He puts his half smoked spliff in the ashtray and goes to his DVD cabinet, he takes out all the superhero movies to see if he can remember a face, but it's useless he only has vague memories of them. He then thinks, I won't have to wait long anyway I'm going to see them all tonight, as he flicks through the movies he starts to laugh and he wonders who will turn up, the Hulk, Mr. fantastic, Superman, and the girls, he can't wait to see the girls, he always had a crush for Emma frost but he can't remember what she looks like ether. He puts the DVD's away goes into his bedroom and to the safe; he takes out a nice bag of Dutch green because he's nearly finished the rocky. The sun has risen fully now and its getting mighty hot, just the fuckin ticket. He strolls back to the veranda and has a blimp at the surf, fuckin looks good to me he thinks, one last quick hour or so in the surf and then I'll get ready. He knock's himself a nice fat green spliff, for the beach, pre-surf whammy, pours himself another Remi and downs it, grabs his surfboard and he's off.

Wales Cardiff 2009

Mel or Storm if you like did turn the colour of boiled shite but that could of been the drugs also, because after she read the letter (and forgot almost instantly in her next-day-drug-fuelled-mind) she remembered she was holding the rabbit, she turns and spots her two skunk joints on the table, the letter hits the floor and she hits the couch, her knickers are off and the joints in her mouth, then she decides, before I start I think I'll do myself a Jack Daniels and diet coke, after she has poured her delicious beverage she puts a porno on, she's not bothered which one just as long as there's a nice healthy cock to look at, then the spliff is back in her mouth, what a fantastic sight to behold, Storm lying on the couch with her legs spread, rubbing the vibrating rabbit on her pussy button and toking on a joint. Fucking priceless, the next morning when she wakes she has a hazy weird idea something happened, she knows what happened to herself because the rabbit is still in her pussy and there's a half smoked joint on her belly, (good job she'd put the ashtray on the table.) but there's something else, something niggling at her, like when you think you've gone out and left the fire on, that's when she sits bolt up and looks at the letter on the floor, fuck me, it all comes back in a mass flurry, she picks the letter up and gives it a second gander, it's not that long and also it doesn't say who it's from, wow the marvellous, she hasn't thought of these guys for years, she's finding it hard to remember who was actually in the marvellous, she remembers Mystique because she was her best friend, they said they'd stay in touch but she remembers Superman being a prick on this point, (no we mustn't tell anybody about ourselves and we must never meet up) well somebody did she's thinking, because of all them comic books and movies, she'd love to meet Stan and ask him how he knew, she starts to get a bit excited about meeting her old friends, she has a quick glance at the calendar just to check it won't clash with her Ibiza stint, but in her head although she's still hazy she already knows she'll be cool for the trip, and then just like a woman its pack time dilemma, but then just like a space cadet, she thinks fuck it I'm taking everything, she doesn't have to take any toys like most of the boys do, but her clobber takes up three jumbo suitcases, she decides to have a quick munch and a nice coffee because she still feels a little delicate, then it's in the shower for the scrub up, she must have gave her fanny some hammering last night because it's still a bit tender, but she's soon done and looking a million bucks. Because she's a raver it's a fucking must have to own a beetle, but she didn't want an old one because their pretty uncomfortable, so she was fuckin dancing when the new ones came out, so as most of the marvellous do, she went all out, she got a pink custom Turbo S cabriolet, the fastest beetle on the road, and pimped out to fuck, pink Recaro seats pink leather interior, and the rest polished chrome, she's even got a darker pink Aztec tattoo on the exterior front wings, so you can just about see it, its fuckin sweet, she's also got a Jaguar XKR convertible. She's not arsed which car she should take, it depends more on which car is better for the cases, she picks the beetle for fun more than anything and the cases go in ok, she taps the post code into the satnav, right then she's thinking, this is it, this is it, time to meet the old crew.

Edinburgh Scotland 2009

Once Lysa or mystique if you want, had read the letter she was about to show the Adonis the door, then she thought fuck it, if I'm going to be out of town for a while I might as well get me hole once more before I go, and the Adonis did not disappoint, his cock wasn't the biggest shed ever had but it certainly filled a hole, he was like a little Irish mush digging holes for fun, each time he slid his length in it took her breath away, so by mid-afternoon she had showed him the door and was thinking of the month to come, and the friends she hadn't seen for over a century, she's so excited she nearly pisses herself, (this could also have something to do with the Adonis leaving her fanny feeling and looking like a fuckin big Mac) after she sorts out a month's worth of clothes and packs, it's out with the comic's and DVD's so she can do a bit of reminiscing. She remembers her old friend storm the most, but what anyone looks like is beyond her. She can remember the Hulk for one reason and one reason only, not his face or what his amazing personality was like, but just the size of his cock when he changed, yes even then she had a thing for the well-endowed man, but she was shy and prudish then, but the Hulk had something completely different, apart from it being green it was like a wall of flesh, in fact it was so big it actually looked like a cartoon dick, and the veins, the veins were like fingers running down to his bell end. This is what got her more excited than anything else, she knew he'd be there, and now she was all woman and no little shy girl, as she's watching the DVD's she ponders who could have written the letter and asked her to come to this manor house, she has a vague idea it will be Superman, he was always the organiser. Lysa has only got one car and she renews it every year, she has the Mercedes-Benz SLR McLaren convertible in silver with red interior, she hasn't got room for her clothes so she packs a small bag and gets a courier to drop by and pick up her cases, the courier that came was quite tasty and any other time she might of give him a go, she's all sorted now so she's planned to set off first thing in the morning, she's got the post code she just needs to pop it in the satnav.

Birmingham 2009

Blade or Brian to us, (like all the others) has had a day and all night to ponder the current situation. He's very excited, he's going to miss his kids but he's only going for a month, he's told the oldest and most trustworthy of the clan, and that would be Andy, that he's rented the sports hall and all their equipment for them, they can practice for as long as they like every day, all day. He hasn't seen his friends in a long time and he's looking forward to the reformation of the clan, he's seen his own movies fuckin loads of times so he didn't need to watch them again, and all them Spiderman movies can fuck right off, he can't believe they depicted that cunt as a good guy, he fuckin hates the cunt, so he put on the fantastic four, he chooses the second one, the rise of the Silver Surfer, because he remembers him, the Silver Surfer that is, and he also remembers the day he died, it's a bit depressing but he remembers him fondly, he knows if he had lived they would of become great friends, the Silver Surfer is one of the super beings that Brian remembers properly, probably because they got on so well, he remembers there was a Mr fantastic but can't remember what he looks like, and he remembers Superman, he was a pushy fucker, he's the one who probably sent this letter, he's trying to remember the girls, but he can only remember Storm because he fancied the ass off her, he remembers she was fit as fuck, and when that group came out Skunk Anansie he couldn't believe the resemblance, he actually thought it was her for a while. He's packed all his gear and like Sid he's only going to bring clothes, and cameras, O and his iPod and portable speakers, loads of chill out gear and a couple of suits, he loves his suits, he's got a Brioni, a Kiton, a Canali, and a Bottega Veneta, he knows he's only going for a month and that's if he stays that long, but you never know, so he's going to throw in his Issey Miyake one just in case, you know what they say it's better to have a condom and not need it, than to need one and not have it. Brian doesn't need to think about cars and what he's going to drive down to the manor in, there's only one choice his Maserati Gran Turismo S, it's black, and a fuckin beauty, it's even got black wheels. His suits get hung on the suit hangers in the back, his bags go in the boot, the iPod goes on, Eminem starts blasting out, (O...OO...OOOO..O..O I'm as cold as the cold wind blo..bb..blow..bb blow blows) Brains head starts bobbing as he punches the post code into the sat nav and the fuckers off.

Chelsea London 2009

Emma after first shiting herself for five minutes, calmed down and thought fuck it I will go out, she wouldn't have the chance to show off her dress to the girls for a month or so, and everything was out and ready to go, plus after all that work on her pussy jungle, no way was she missing out, and was she glad, you fuckin better believe it, the girls were green as fuck, and she was delighted, she was so delighted she forgot all about the letter and got slaughtered with the girls, she remembers the next morning though, she didn't know how she felt about it and to tell the truth she really didn't feel anything, she hasn't thought about any of them for years, and I mean years. The only one she can vaguely remember is the Sandman and that's only because she had a crush on him. Even when the comic books first came out she never gave them a second glance, she remembers just giving a little laugh when she first seen the Hulk on TV in the seventies, and only because she knew the truth. A few giggles now and then at new movies like Superman and Spiderman, but other than that she never gave a fuck, in fact now that she thinks about it she never even thought about how whoever wrote the story's knew what they knew, she always assumed that Stan Lee was an alias for one of them who decided to make a few bob, how else would he know, so as I said she just didn't give a fuck. She just got on with her life; she also hasn't given a thought as to who wrote the letter and if she did, (yes you guessed it she wouldn't give a fuck.) So now she's wondering what to take, and she's thinking fuck it I'm taking everything, well the letter did say it's a stately manor so I'm taking the lot. She starts to pack and orders a crew of specialty movers for her clothes, she doesn't give a fuck about anything else. She's looking into the walk-in wardrobe and thinking this cunt manor house better have one of these or I'm coming straight back home, I've only just got back into town and now I've got to fuck off again. Emma is a bit like Brian or Blade when it comes to cars, and just like everything else she doesn't give a fuck, she just went out and bought the best, a fuckin Bugatti Veyron sang noir super sport special edition in white pearl with aluminium side wings, when the man dropped it off outside her apartment she actually got a bit excited, it was one of the most beautiful things she'd ever seen, she almost had a tear in her eye, and even now every time she sees it she actually gets a twinge in her fanny, so once the movers have been and gone she puts her small but expensive case in the back and all she has to do is put the post code in the sat nav, set up her iPod, and she's off.

The Cave 2009.

The boss Magneto sits in his cave looking at a huge wall of screens that are playing out every room in the manor house, but he is brooding again when he should feel joy. The Marvellous are falling into his trap and he will soon get the revenge he has dreamed of for over a century. If the Marvellous do not join with him and his plan, so be it, they will die. So, he is brooding but only for the loss of his old friends, friends he knows would be celebrating with him now if they were here, but they're not, they're all dead, well nearly all, except for those here and her, wherever she is. When the Marvellous disbanded and disappeared most of his friends went on crazy rampages, killing humans and taking their belongings, these creatures were hunted down, then tortured and killed, they have now fallen into the web of history and legend, the big foot, the yeti, the lizard man, but Magneto, Sabretooth and his friend Jack and her could see their downfall enfolding and fled to England, they lost jack on the crazy docks of London, it was like a fuckin zoo back then he remembers, then a few days later he sees a newspaper, the front page jumped out at him. (SPRING HEELED JACK SEEN IN CITY) O bollocks he thought that's him done, he kept his eye on the papers for the next few days but nothing else accrued, then a week later another. (SPRING HEEL JACK COUGHT IN LIVERPOOL) they had chased him all the way from London to Liverpool and he hadn't even committed a crime, Magneto was furious, they killed him for nothing, because he was different. This is when he swore to rid the planet of the human race, they are despicable, they kill and mutilate everything and anything that they come across, they even slaughter themselves, yes, this world will be better without these cockroaches. So, Magneto and Sabretooth retreat to the hills, were Magneto could use his powers to build them a fortress where they could plot and plan for the future. As with all the super beings money was never a problem, if you never had it you just took it. Magneto for the first twenty to thirty years built his domain and kept up with the events of the times, always on the lookout for strange stories or weird occurrences, this is how he found his partner in crime and best friend Ra's al Ghul, they came together in nineteen hundred and ten and have plotted together ever since. Ra's al Ghul brought with him Spiderman who immediately bonded and felt the strongest loyalty for his new boss Magneto. Together the four of them have plotted the downfall of the marvellous and the human race, "we will leave just a few thousand of these beings alive to serve our purposes, and if the Marvellous do not want to join us then they will die ha, ha, ha". And so, began the search for the Marvellous, they knew Superman would not and could not be found so they left him out for they knew as soon as they captured the others he would come to them. And so, they focused on the others. Nobody not even the Marvellous knew that they had all come to England, but what a fantastic stroke of luck this turned out to be for the not so marvellous. As the years trickled by and people became easier to find they were getting closer, then one glorious day out of the blue comic books started to appear on the shelves, describing each and every one of them in detail, again some of it was false or twisted truths but it was them all the same, it had occurred to Magneto to locate this Stan Lee and ask for himself how he knew these things, for he disliked his comic book persona, and Spiderman utterly despised his, but they knew America was not the place to be looking, it was England, and they were right, Stan Lee would have to wait. It wasn't hard for the genus of Spiderman to locate them all, the only one they still hadn't found was Superman. The only conclusion to make was that he was dead or that Superman was Stan Lee, so he sent her back to America to find this Stan Lee and find out the truth once and for all, but it did not matter now anyway, they had the one that really mattered here and that was the Hulk, every superhero can be killed or made to submit, but not the Hulk, the Hulk is the key to the Marvellous, nothing can destroy him and nobody can hurt him, even Superman is shit scared of him because he is the only living thing which could almost or even maybe kill Superman. When the Hulk is in Hulk out mode he is truly invincible. This is the key to Magneto's plan; he wants to know what has happened to the Marvellous over the years, how they have used their powers, if at all, and how they now see the human race, they want to see how living with humans has affected these heroes. His good friend Ra's al Ghul comes into the room with a tray in hand, "hello my friend I thought we'd celebrate with a glass of the best" on the tray are two beautiful Waterford crystal siren brandy glasses and a diamond encrusted bottle of Henri IV Dudognon, the pair of them glance at each other with great smirks on their faces, "so they are arriving as we speak" say's Ra al Ghul, he's looking at the screen as he pours out two glasses, the Hulk has just come into his bedroom, they look at each other again and shake heads as the Hulk attempts to put up his framed picture of the Liverpool waterfront. They both sit back in their magneto-made relaxo chairs, Ra al Ghul pulls a joint out of his top pocket and sparks it up, as the purple smoke and beautiful aroma fill the room Ra al Ghul passes the reefer to Magneto, "this my friend is going to be one extremely eventful month".

The Manor. 2009 First arrivals

An Audi R8 Spider V10 glides across the gravel pathway of the manor house; its roof is down, both Dave and H are ogling the manor, this is fuckin massive say's the Hulk, look at the fuckin size of it. Dave's proper impressed also, and as his eyes scan the manor, he's full of awe, "this is a fuckin beaut mate, and you were worried that all ye stuff wouldn't fit" says Dave smiling at H. The manor house is fuckin huge and the Audi's the only car there. "We must be the first ey" says Dave. "Yer looks like it". "Do ye wana do the honours on the front door H", "do ye recon that's what the keys for" asks H, "must be kid". Dave and H approach the front doors of the manor and there's a strange key swipe on the wall. "Go on kid swipe it", the Hulk swipes the key and the front doors open in. There's no creaky hinges or anything but it still looks a bit spooky, they are greeted by a huge marble tiled hall. "This is fuckin plush mate" Dave's voice echoes around the marble hallway as he looks around, "am fuckin made up we got here first kid, we get first dibs on the rooms". Dave and H go sprinting through the house to see who can get the best room but give in after five minutes when they realise every room is fuckin huge, it doesn't matter which room you have. H goes back outside to the car to get their small bags as their wagon comes up the driveway. "Fuckin good timin that boys" shouts H, he's made up because he can get his gear in now before anyone else arrives. H reluctantly lets the lads from the removal company help him, but not before giving them a stern warning. "Anyone puts a fuckin scratch on anything there'll be fuckin murders. And don't even think about touchin the guitars am the only cunt that touches them". Dave grabs his few bags and he's off to his room to set up his gear, he spotted a good room before with a boss plasma so that he can play his games in bed, he's setting up his platstation3 and his WII can go downstairs, he saw a big telly in the communal room (well that's what he's named it, it's a massive room to the right of the main hall and it connects to the kitchen so it's defo the communal room.) H goes to the kitchen to see what's in and is fuckin flabbergasted, "there's every food under the sun in here" he's shouting to Dave, "and bevy's mush, every type of bevy there's wines, lagers, and every type of short you can get", he's doing the removal lads a cuppa before they go for doing such a good job. Once the coffee's dished out he goes to his room to have a gander, WOW his room looks fuckin boss, all his boards are in their hangers, his big photo of Liverpool waterfront is up on the wall, his guitars are out of their bags and on their stands, fuck me they look good, he always nearly gets a stiffy when he sees his guitars out like this. His electrical stuff is out but not hooked up, so he decides to do it. He chose a room with only a little TV on his side board, and that's so he can blast his 3D projector on to the nice white wall. He turns it on to test, now that's a fuckin telly he's thinking, seven feet across, every cunt's gona be jealous of this. Dave shouts H down to see the moving men go. As they stand on the step watching the removal van turning out of the manor, an absolute fucking dream car turns onto the drive, the gravel pathway that leads to the manor is quite long so they get a good gander as the silver Aston Martin DBS goes cruising past. H looks at his little Audi next to this beast and thinks, I should have brought the Q7, but his little baby still looks the biz. Dave is speechless, the car looks like a fuckin tank. H breaks the silence and the jealous tension. "Fuckin kip of him kid, look at his fuckin sidey's, he thinks he's the real fuckin Wolverene". Dave's pissing himself but trying not to make it to obvious. The crazy fucker with the sidey's is looking out of the side window with a massive cheesy grin on his face as he cruses past. "Fuckinhell, I don't remember this cunt he looks like a fuckin loon to me" Says the Hulk from the side of his mouth. Wolverine pulls up next to H's Audi, he has a little look at H's car and although the Audi is shit hot, Brian thinks he's won the war of the best car, he turns off the engine and jumps out full of enthusiasm, "now then the lads, fuckin long time no see", Wolverine walks towards the boys with his hand outstretched, "you're Mr. fantastic and you're the Hulk, Right", H and Dave look at each other, then look back at Brian, they can't believe his accent, it's a very sweet timid Geordie accent and doesn't go with his sidey's at all. "err ye mate that's us, am Dave an this is H, so you must be Wolverine then, I kinda guessed by the sidey's kid". H has to turn and tries not to laugh. "Yer right man that's me like, my names Brian now, a canny believe your scouser's like, av you been livin in Liverpool all this time". The Hulk buts in now with his bullish scouse voice, "ye mate we av, an you're from Newcastle ay, would ye fuckin believe it, all this time an we only live up the road from each other". As the guys are getting acquainted a wagon comes around the corner and up the drive, "it's all my stuff man" says Brian, "we'll let you get settled in then mate, were gona be in the kitchen avin a coffee when ye want us kid". They leave Brian alone to order his men around. Brian can't believe the size of the manor, the reception hall is like a footy pitch, he goes upstairs and checks the rooms out, I bet them two fuckers av took the best rooms, but he's delighted when he sees that all the rooms are massive, they're all different though some have small TV's and some massive. All have a huge bed and an on-suite bathroom. Brian is well chuffed, there's enough room in here to set up all his gym gear. When he gets downstairs H and Dave are in the communal room, Dave is setting up a Nintendo WII. "We'll av some fuckin laugh's wid this ay kid", he say's as Brian comes in. H is sitting on the couch looking out the window. "No ye prick" he says to Dave, should av brought me X Box with the motion trakin shit an that". Dave scoffs, "fuckoff, the Wii's well better, old skool kid old skool". H turns and asks Brian what he wants to drink, "ad love a coffee like", "no problem mucka" say's H, just as H is going to get up from the couch he freezes and starts chuckling saying, "ayy up, av a fuckin gander at this", from H's position at the window he can see to the end of the drive and he just spotted a fuckin pimped out pink beauty turning the corner. They all run outside at full sprint, nearly knocking each other over and come to a halt on the step as Storm rumbles past, the pink roof of her Beetle Turbo S is down, and some old top buzz CD is thumping out, she's beaming at the boys. "Now then the lads" she shouts as she goes past. The boys are nearly drooling, they don't remember her being this fit, she slides up next to brains DBS, and has a little peep at the boy's cars, "mmmm very nice" she purrs as the door opens and her massive long chiselled legs come creeping from the car. "So, which one of you lovely gentlemen are going to help me with my bags?" The three lads glance at each other, and then simultaneously three hands shoot up into the air. Mel has a little giggle, Brian, fuckin geek as always buts in, "a canny believe it man, it's the one and only storm in the flesh". "Yer, hi guys" says storm looking a little embarrassed, "I was storm but you can call me Mel now". H walks past giving Brian the evil eye, what a fuckin bell end he thinks as he picks two of Mel's cases out of the car, "nice little motor that luv, my names H and I was the Hulk back in the day", "OOO yer I can kind of remember yer face now", lies Mel as she gives H a little peck on the cheek, Dave's arm shoots out like a bolt of lightning for the other case so he can get himself one of those smackeroos, it's back at his side but she's gone leading H up the stairs to find a room, Dave runs after them thinking I'll get one in the bedroom. Brian is about to follow when he hears the familiar crunch of the gravel driveway, a silver Mersedes-benz SLR McLaren rumbles up the drive, its roof is down and Brian could see a girl, he knew from memory it was Mystique his old flame, he decides not to shout the others, he wants to go Hans solo into this mission. Lysa rolls her car next to Mel's and has a little glance across the line of cars, "mmmm some nice motas here I must say". Brian has come over to meet her, "you must be Mystique, I'm Brian I used to be", "Wolverine" shouts Lysa before he can say it, "yer that's right do you remember me then". (Brian is over the fuckin moon Mystique the love of his past remembers him). "No sorry I don't, ye jist look like him is all, ye no, the movie you", Brian is a bit deflated and a bit embarrassed. "My names Lysa Brian it's nice to meet you again, is there anyone else here, there's a few cars here already", "yer there's a few love, Storms just got here, the Hulk and Mr fantastic are just helping her up to her room", "Storm, Storm's here", Lysa nearly knocks Brian over as she shoots in to find her old friend, plus she defo heard the Hulk is also upstairs, she fly's up the stairs and leaves Brian on the porch. She hears the laughter coming from one of the rooms and bursts in. Lysa and Mel look at each other and do the high-pitched scream as they run into each other's arms, there still screaming as they try and tell each other their new names, H and Dave are looking at each other with James Bond eyebrows and big cheesy grins, "would you like a drink of anything girls", asks Dave, "a coffee or a tea", "OO yes please say the girls like two twins", "coffee for me" says Mel, "and me too please" says Lysa. Lysa gives H the once over, and she's well pleased. She looks him straight in the eye and says, "so H I dinny member you being a sexy little fucker", H goes beetroot, but manages to compose himself. "Yer not to bad yeself Lysa love, the years av been kind to ye ay". The girls burst out laughing shaking their heads at H. The boys go back down stairs, H with a massive ego grin, and leave the girls to catch up. Brian is in the communal room watching the TV. "Fuckinell Brian I completely forgot about you kid, why didn't ye come up" says

H as he goes through to the kitchen. "Them birds up there are fuckin mental mate, fuckin screaming their heads off they are", "ay Bri" says Dave "ye might get that cuppa now kid, just as long as no one else turns up", "coffee wasn't it mush" asks H, "yer thanks mate" he says looking at Dave with a smile. "Wha do you want kid" he asks Dave, "coffee please mush", Dave sits on the rap-around sofa, he puts his arm across the back, flops his head back and assumes the chill out position, he turns and looks at Brian, "ay Bri that Lysa birds got a little wet on for me mucka over there, said he was fit, fuckin little live wire she is mate". Brian is not amused he doesn't think he's going to like this H character, so when H comes in with a nice cup of fresh ground coffee for Brian and Dave, Brian has to check himself, seems a nice fella actually he thinks.

North pole 2009 Superman's Crystal Palace.

Superman has been thinking for days, contemplating what he should do. He's been through all the thought patterns, should I go out, shouldn't I go out, am I afraid, am I brave, are my friends in danger, or are these feelings nothing more than paranoia. He's admitted to himself that he's a shit house, and yes, he's shit-scared to go out, and yes, he's certain that his friends are in trouble. He's never had a feeling like this, he thinks it's a part of his powers but doesn't know how it works. And on the subject of powers he doesn't even know if he can fly, he hasn't done it for years, (he keeps forgetting the time his mother and father made him get the satellites and TV's fitted, it was so traumatic he blocked it out) but you know, once you can ride a bike you never forget. He goes into the big room for a few practice runs, he's a bit wobbly at first but soon gets into the swing, he starts giggling to himself, he forgot how much fun this was. He pretends he's sitting in a chair like a sky diver, and then starts doing the silly Russian dance where he folds his arms and kicks his legs out, he even starts to sing the song, dum dum, dum dum, dum dum, dar ra, he floats back down to earth felling pretty confident and jabs the air like Mohamed Ali, ba bam. He goes over and gives himself a look in the mirror; he also looks exactly the same as he always did. The weird thing about superman is that he looks exactly like the superman we all know and love, he's tall about six four, great physique, massive shoulders, six pack pocking through the suit, big blue eyes, he's even got the black hair with the little quiff at the front, and he's got that big sticky out chest thing going on. He's looking, no sorry, he's admiring his superman suit and wondering if still after all these years how it works, (the suit also is exactly the suit we all know and love.) The suit is a marvel of science in itself, nothing, and I mean nothing can mark or tarnish the suit, it's nearly as indestructible as superman, you could throw paint at it or spray paint, and it just falls straight off. You can even piss in it and it soaks it up and spills it out on the other side, and he should know, he's tried it all. He laughs to himself again as he remembers the movie superman three, he's given a piece of weird kryptonite that turns him into a crack-tooting alcoholic, and then he shags that blond bird. He's laughing because in the movie his suit gets all covered in oil and that would never happen. He's decided now is the time to go see his mother and father and tell them he is leaving, he feels confident as he walks into the crystal room, the white stripes are blasting out from the TV, Jack white is singing broken bricks, his mother and father look like Jimmy off Quadrophenia when he's dancing to Louie, Louie, pouted snarly mouths, their eyes are closed and their heads are bobbing like a pair of chicken's. "Mother father shouts Superman I have news for you". Jor-el doesn't stop dancing or open his eyes as he says, "you know the rules dickhead, wait until the songs finished". Superman doesn't wait as he usually would. "I see you are back to your usual self today father, well this is good, for I have good news for you. I am going away, I'm going to England to find my friends". Jor-el and Lara's eyes open and nearly pop out of their heads, but not really because their holograms, "I am not going to wait here for your insults, goodbye". And with that Superman swoops out of the room in flight. Jor-el and Lara are immediately doing high fives and high tens, and whooping to each other, for over a hundred years they've had that boring bastard droning on and on and on, now they are free, free of the fucker, and free to watch as much and whatever TV they want in absolute peace. That is until they hear the generator go off, and all goes dark and quiet, "THAT LITTLE FUCKER".

The Manor, 2009 late arrivals

H has just given the boys their drinks and is about to take the girls drinks upstairs when they come into the room, "hi guys and how are you doing" says Lysa in a sexy Marilyn Monroe voice, H is beaming and gives her the James Bond eyebrows, "I was just gona bring you these" says H, "get yeselves comfy girls", the girls settle into the massive couch and start chatting shit, as H is placing the coffee down he's looking out of the window. "Now that is fuckin nice" says H, all the others turn, they're all looking out the window as a black Maserati Gran turismo S, goes crawling by. Dave looks at H "fuckin beauty that mate init". The car crunches in next to the Mercedes Benz, "fuckin hell" says H, "it's even got black wheels kid, look at them", Brian tries to join in, although he is feeling a bit jealous, his cars still definitely the best one there, "yer it's a fuckin beauty alright" says Brian, H looks Brian straight in the eyes with a menacing look on his face, Brian shits himself for a minute because H looks like he's going to kill him, but then H leans in and says, "not as good as yours though mate is it, yours is well the best car here", Brian is fucking delighted and relieved, he fuckin loves this H character. The girls are chatting shit again about who they think it is, and they find out in the weirdest way ever. It plays out like a movie, they hear the music first as the car door opens, it's the Missy Elliott song hot boyz, there's a deep thumping bass as blade or Brian steps from the car, he looks as though he's walking in slow motion as a blast of wind from nowhere swoops his matrix coat up and out behind him, he looks like the assassin number one from the afro samurai cartoon, missy's silky voice is singing "hot boyz….baby you got….what I want" as Brian gets closer to the manor, H turns to Dave and says, "ay kid is he goin in slow mow or is it my eyes", Dave and Brian have a little giggle, "he fuckin does mush ye, but I tell ye what, he's cool as fuck mush inny", H agrees, he does look cool as fuck. The girls have a mischievous little glance at each other and give each other the, ooooo he's hot faces, Brian comes into the communal room and gives them all a massive smile, they can't believe their ears when the sweetest brummy voice says, "or roight guys am Brian I used to be Blade". all the usual wow's and arr's go around and everybody introduces themselves, missy Elliott can still be heard but low, Brian or Blade pulls his sleeve up and presses stop on his iPod, Dave and H both look at each other then back at Brian or Blade, "what the fucks that Bri" says H, "o yer boss this mate, I got an iPod on me arm that goes into a tiny Bose speaker on me back", Dave and H both look at each other again, and like Siamese twins say, "that is cooool as fuck mate", but then, H jumps up, he gives both the Brains a good look over and says, "how the fuck lads, out of all the names in the world, did you two pick the same fuckin name", he points at Brian and says "Brian your Bri", then he points at Blade and says "Brian you B", B says "well yow can just call me Blade if you want guys, its only us here init", "fair doos Blade mate, saves any confusion dunit mate, and err what do ye want to drink big fella" says H, "orr I'll have a coffee ployse H", the girls by now are back glued to the window and talking more shit, they suddenly get excited as girls do and start squealing, "there's somebody coming, there's somebody coming". A beautiful white BMW X6 comes crawling up the drive, with that beautiful pop and ping sound a gravel driveway makes, it pulls in next to the Maserati. A little guy gets out, pops the boot and grabs a big suitcase, as he's getting his case from the boot he hears the gravel popping again and looks down the drive to see a navy-blue Audi TT RS Roadster crunching up the drive, the sandman pulls in next to the invisible man, the sandman gets out and also pops the boot to get his bags, not that you can fit much in an Audi TT but he has stuff on the back seat also. "Or right mate I'm Sid" says the invisible man with his hand stretched out, "I used to be the invisible man". "All right mate I'm Brodi I used to be the Sandman". After having a quick envious glance at the row of supercars the guys shake hands and turn to the manor with their bags only to see five faces glued to the window looking at them. "That must be the rest of the guys then" says Brodi as they walk to the door. Back in the communal room H comes from the kitchen with Blades coffee. "I can't fuckin believe you cunts, yer all sittin there lookin out the window, and not one of yuz has gone to open the door for them, fuckin gang of lazy bastards" says H as he goes for the front door. The others hear H at the front door, "now then lads come in, put ye cases in the hall for now lads, get yeselves a nice cuppa first, am H boys I used to be the Hulk". H is pumping the lad's hands as he ushers them into the communal room. The invisible man and the Sandman enter the room with the same five faces looking up at them. "Ow wight guys I'm Sid, I used to be the invisible man" says Sid in his deep cockney accent. "Hi guys I'm Brodi and I am the Sandman" says Brodi in his none-accented voice, Brodi hasn't really got an accent from all the travelling he does, there's a slight bit of a Cornish twang but you have to have a keen ear to hear it, he sounds more like Connor Mccloud from the movie highlander. H didn't see them driving in and spy's a very sexy Audi through the window, "wow who's is the TT lads, that's fuckin sweet" says H, "that's mine mate" reply's Brodi, "do you like Audis then H" asks Brodi, "to fuckin right I do kid, that's mine on the end there" says H as he points out of the window at his Audi R8. "That's a fuckin beauty mate you'll have to give us a go of that later", H is fuckin delighted, he's well chuffed he didn't bring the Q7, "fuckin to right Brodi mate I'll go on the net and see if there's any race tracks close by and we can all go and race our cars there, it'll be a fuckin scream". "Is there an internet connection here then H" asks Lysa, "yer love when I sorted me room out before, I started me lap top up and it went straight on the net so it must be wireless'ed up". H turns to the two newcomers. "Sorry boys I forgot to ask you if you want a drink" says H, "what would you like lads"; "just coffee would be fine thanks" answer the boys. "I might as well do another full round then, does everybody want another one ye". Everyone shouts yes at H as he disappears into the kitchen, "aarr he's a sweetie pie is that one" says Mel, Dave stretches his eyes supper wide and gives her a look of mock shock surprise, "yev only just met him though babe, give him a few hours and you'll be callin him all the cunts under the sun". Every ones laughing as H pops his head round the door, "I hope ye not all laughin at me ye gang of cunts, yez can do yer own fuckin coffee", he says with his little cheeky grin. H brings the drinks in and everyone's gabbing, chatting shit and catching up when a couple of courier vans pull onto the driveway, "that will be my gear" says Mel, and just like a woman she rushes out all excited to see all her own clothes. There's another van, well more like a seven and a half tone wagon, with what looks like the full Milan fashion show on board, Mel goes back in and asks whose it is, nobody knows? "Well its deffo some girls" says Mel, Lysa just looks at her and shrugs her shoulders, "not mine honey". Brodi buts in, "I think I know whose it is, Emma frost isn't here yet it could be hers, I'll go and take it off the wagon for her, but it'll have to stay out there until she gets here". So, Mel goes out with Brodi and H follows to give a hand, (more like have a good mooch at what's in the van) they take all Mel's gear out of her van first and it goes straight up to her room for her, lucky for them there's not that much, they come back down and the courier guys have taken everything out of the van, "fuckin hell look at all that clobber" says H as they all stand in amazement looking at the clothes. They're just about to start to ferry them in, the courier vans have gone when the familiar sound of the gravel driveway draws their attention to the end of the drive. H does a flying u turn back into the manor and comes screaming into the communal room, "COME AND AV A FUCKIN GANDER AT THIS". Everybody jumps up and goes sprinting outside, the next thing you hear is a chorus of oooss and wows and fuckinell's as one of the most beautiful cars in the world goes crawling past. "Now that, is what I call a fucking car my friends" says H as the white Bugatti Vayron slides in next to the Audi TT. Emma is looking out of her window and laughing at the faces of pure astonishment, she climbs out happy to be the centre of attention. H walks over and introduces himself as he takes a walk around the car giving it the once over. "This is fuckin sweet babe, how fuckin much did this set ye back" he says as he runs his fingers over the immaculate paint job and onto the chrome. "Never you mind curly top" says Emma as she gives H a cheeky smile. The massive front drive of the manor now looks like a top gear special, Jeremy Clarkson would be cumming in his pants if he was there, the line of cars reads something like this, an Audi R8, Aston Martin, Beetle turbo, Mercedes Benz, Maserati, BMW X6, Audi TT, and a Bugatti at the end, H steps out and looks along the line of cars, he does a little whistle "wwwwoooo that's some fuckin line o cars that is mate". All H can think is, am fuckin takin all these fuckers out for a spin, am fuckin straight on the net for a nice little race track. Brodi comes over and although it's been over one hundred years he still feels that same twinge he did back then, "hi Emma I'm Brodi", he says as he gives her a little peck on the cheek, "I remember you honey" says Emma, "you're the Sandman I used to have a crush for you back in the days". Wow, now Brodi feels more than a twinge as H gives him a playful dig in the ribs, "get in there ye hansom devil", H looks at Emma "now let's get all your stuff up to your room and we can all get to know each other again". Emma gives all the other guys a wave and shouts over, "hi guys I'm Emma and I used to be Emma frost the ice queen, I'm glad you're all here actually cos I forgot me key card thing", they all start to trundle off inside, but with all the lads seeming to lag back a little and take a bit longer, this probably has something to do with the fact that Emma has the fittest ass you've ever seen, and the boys want to have a good gander at it, Dave and H give each other another look and as H points to the tremendous globe that's climbing the stairs they mouth a silent fuckinell what an ass at each other. Brodi sees this and gives them and older brother scowl as he shakes his head, but he's laughing really, he doesn't care, he's high as a kite on the fact that she remembers him, and as he gives that tremendous ass a little look himself, he can't help thinking as men do, I might be looking at that soon, bent over with her big fat blond doughnut sticking out inviting me in. Dave stops at the doors of the manor and has a look back at the cars, H sees his mucka looking at the line of beauties, he comes over and puts his arm around Dave and gives him a mucka crunch, "am getting on the net in a minute kid, to find a fuckin boss race track, an were gona rag the fuck out of every one of them" says H with the biggest cheese grin, Dave turns to H and gives him one back, but inside he's a bit scared, he's been on a race track with H before and remembers how much of a fuckin lunatic he was, he's sure he remembers saying he'd never do it again, but then again it is a sweet fuckin line o cars. "Come on kid" says H "let's put the fuckin kettle on ay.

The Cave 2009.

A good few hours have passed since we were last in the cave and the mood has changed somewhat, Magneto is now in great spirits, he's forgotten all about his old friends and the depression the image of them brought. There are now four of them watching the screens but let's backtrack slightly, sabretooth came down first when he smelt the fumes from the joint that was getting passed between Magneto and Ra's al Ghul, it was a sweet smelling bud from the dam called laughing Buddha and Ra's al Ghul had a pocket full of them, Ra's al Ghul was felling fantastic, he knew why his friend had been sad, he was grieving for are lost brothers and frets for her, he fears something has happened to her, but now was not the time for brooding, now is the time for rejoice and revenge, he knew the joint and brandy would chill the boss out, it was going to be a good day, "ah Sabretooth" says Magneto "let me pull up a chair for you and come get yourself a glass of this", he holds up his glass of Dudognon brandy and gives Sabretooth the face that says, this is fuckin tasty, a bit like the face that Harvey Keitel gives Quentin Tarantino in pulp fiction when he gives Harvey some good coffee. Sabretooth makes himself comfortable with his brandy and not before long he's chugging on a nice spliff of the laughing Buddha, this pleasantness does not last long for Sabretooth unfortunately because soon enough Spiderman comes in to join the party. Sabretooth is absolutely gutted and is having thoughts of leaving the party but Spiderman is also in good spirits and for once, just once, they get along laughing at the screens and the antics of the Marvellous. So now we have all four super villains, all in the chairs that the boss Magneto made, it's a massive clump of metal and somehow Magneto has made the inside soft and the outside firm so they basically have the same effect as a memory foam mattress, they mould perfectly to the person's body shape, a fucking fantastic invention by the way and the most comfortable chair in the world. So, they have brandy in one hand, joint in the other, enjoying the show. It's a bit like watching big brother, watching them all meet up again and finally all go in the manor house, it's totally not what any of them were expecting, the cars, the clothes and the personalities, but what they're all amazed at was the fact that none of them are using their powers, not one, except for a little party trick from Mr Fantastic, have they forgot they have them, or do they just not bother any more, time will tell, it is only early days yet. The main character in this little ensemble is the Hulk whom they have learnt has called himself H, but this does not matter, all that matters are his powers and if he can still change, but up to now things are looking promising, the Hulk is a little pussy cat, Magneto's plan couldn't be running any more perfectly. And then, just when they thought it couldn't get any better, the night time starts to creep in and the Marvellous all start to go off for their first night of alone time in their rooms, and their first night's sleep.

The Manor 2009 first night.

The gang have all settled in the communal room and H is in the kitchen making another tray full of freshly ground coffee, but back in the communal room all eyes are on Dave. The invisible man can't believe how calm and nice H is, all he can remember about him is that he was an absolute lunatic, nobody could control him, even Superman was terrified of him, he whispers at Dave, "oy Dave I can't believe ow fackin nice your mate H is, oy used to be shit scared of him", all the others are nodding, and a little chorus of, fuckin rights and so did I's go around then it's all eyes back on Dave. Dave is having a little chuckle to himself, "yer, ye right guys, when I first got lumbered with um, I shit myself to be honest with ye, but erm, you know, we got into loads of boss stuff and all we do is av a laugh most of the time, so he's sound now, he hasn't tried to hulk out fer years now, but through the years there's been some close ones I can fuckin tell ye". Everyone is nodding and shaking their heads at the same time at the thought of such an ordeal. Brian is captivated, he can't believe the time Dave must have had with H when he's having one of his turns, he can't stop thinking about it, all of the years and years trying to calm him down and get him to the place he is now. "Arr Dave man, says Brian, you'll have to tell us some of the tales mate, aboot all them years in Liverpool, a canny even imagine it mate", "yer I will kid" says Dave "were here for a month mush, loads of time for tales". H comes in with the coffee and dishes them out, everyone's sitting in a kind of half-moon, on a huge wraparound sofa, it's a sofa designed for a home cinema setup so there's a fifty inch plasma on the wall in front of them and a Blu-ray on a shelf below, but it's all turned off and the uncomfortable silence starts to fill the room, everybody's eyes are scanning each other, H shouts it out first and everyone's gutted because they wanted to be the one to ask, but it's H the pushy fucker who asks, "So who was it then, that told Stan Lee about us", they're all smirking and giggling as they look at each other wondering and guessing who it was, H goes first, "well I know for a fact it wasn't me or Dave, so there's us out the picture", Blade jumps in, "arr, it wasn't me ether, av been dying to meet Stan to ask" they all jump in at the same time now with, me too's and so do I's, then the whole room goes quiet and it's Brodi who voices the next dilemma, "so, if none of us here told him about us, who the fuck was it, it could have been one of them bad fuckers or maybe Superman, but that stuck up cunt was always an anal fucker about revealing ourselves" " I remember most of them bad fuckers getting killed off though" says Brian", "yer I can remember a few of them dying as well says Emma", H jumps in with the ice breaker at this point when he says, "who gives a fuck anyway, it's done our fuckin ego's no harm as it", everyone's laughing and agreeing and the mood going good. Emma who hasn't really settled into her room or seen the manor yet asks if everyone else has. "Me Dave and Brian have, we've been ere for ages" says H, "tell ye what guys I'll give ye a tour if ye want". Everyone's up for a tour so off they all go. "You've seen the hall and the communal room so this is the kitchen" says H as he leads them round the manor, "it's just a fuckin kitchen with a good coffee maker to be honest" says H, "so, on we go". He takes them through a door at the other side of the kitchen and the gasps all come at once, they walk into a huge gym fitted out with top of the range equipment, "fuckinell" says Blade "this is fuckin brilliant", Brian has set up all his equipment and the gym looks even better than it did with all new Chinese training equipment, they all start having a go of their favourite exercise, the lads are all clocking the girls asses as they do some very hot workouts, there laughing and giggling, oblivious of the lads drooling, or as crafty birds are, they know exactly what they're doing, "right lets go" shouts H, because he can feel a twinge in his pants and the last thing he needs is a hard on, there's a door on the left side of the gym but they know what's behind it because the wall is completely made of glass looking out to an Olympic size swimming pool. "This is gona be some great month girls" says Emma as they walk around the pool to the outdoor terrace and gardens, the gardens are unbelievable there's about four tiki huts scattered around, a few hot tubs and barbeques, decked areas and polished sandstone paved patios, all the gang are oooing and arrring. "Fuckinhell there's a fuckin tennis court down there" says Brodi, "I man, there's a fuckan basketball court doon there as well" says Brian, "spot on, a little game of one on one tomorrow ay lads", says Brodi, "o yer! What do ye mean lads, can't we fuckin play basketball", says

Mel. Brodi tries to get out of his chauvinistic remark but all he produces is some muttering and spluttering, the lads are pissing themselves. They go back into the pool and head for a door on the other side, H leads them to it as he mouths to the boys, "your gona fuckin love this", when they go through they enter a huge snooker and pool hall, there's a full size snooker table and two pool tables, along the walls are various games, darts, pinball machines, tin-can alley, and some old video games phoenix and track and field, there's even an old sit down video game, and its only fuckin space invaders. The lads are all looking at each other giving it the James Bond eyebrows and mouthing things to each other, such as, fuckin bonanza, get in, fuckin spot on, the girls think it looks alright, but there more interested in a hallway that runs of the games room, there are movie posters all over the hall which leads to a set of double doors, and when they go through they enter a pretty big cinema. Fuckin brilliant shout the girls in unison. "O you fuckin beauty" says Blade as he walks in behind them, "I hope yow's have brought some DVD's", H Dave and Brian have all got cheesy grins again because they know which room their going to next, they go back to the pool and through another door at the end which leads to a huge library, "there must be ten thousand books ere" says Mel, "fuckinhell, says Brodi, look at all these DVD's there's fuckin thousands", "boss" says Mel "there's load of Blu-ray as well", everybody's laughing at Blade whose shaking his head as he laughs, he's looking at the lads, "yow fuckin knew these were all here didn't yow", the lads have a giggle as they all start looking for something to take, they end up with a couple each, H Brian and Dave have already taken theirs earlier so they go through another door which leads back to the hall, all the others follow, "wow" says Emma ""I'm gona fuckin love it here, right guys I'm sorry to just love and leave you but I've got a shit load of unpacking to do, so am fuckin off to me room". Their all shouting goodnight as they file back into the communal room. So as the evening draws in they all start to get a hankering for a tipple, and a few joints of their favourite Smokey, Smokey. They're all a bit cagey about the weed situation as of yet, also they're not so sure of each other, all except Dave and H that is, so one by one they start to make their excuses to disappear to their rooms, Dave's the first and he doesn't need an excuse he just tells it like it is, "right am of to me room for some PlayStation 3 action, am gona pop a beer and spark a nice fuckin big fat one", he does the Cheech thing from up in smoke as he's walking out pretending he's got a joint and it's a zeppelin, "fuck it then if your goin so am I" says H as he jumps up to follow his mucha, "see ye later on then kids, and don't stay up to late he shouts". It doesn't take too long for everyone else to make their excuses to get up to their rooms, Dave's straight into his room and as he said, beer in one hand spliff in the other, and a PlayStation pad in his lap, he's all hooked up to his fifty inch HD plasma, he couldn't be happier, except for the annoying fact that H is next to him waiting to hog his joint, and bending his ear about everyone, "what did ye think of them, who did ye think was fit, what car was the best". H is on a high from meeting them all again, it's been a hectic day, plus he's had about ten coffee's, So Dave does his usual tricks to calm his mate, he swivels round gives his mate a glass of his favourite brandy, and pops a joint in his mouth, ten minutes later H is trying to give Dave a goodnight hug, "come on mucka giz a goodnight hug", "fuckoff ye loon", says Dave as he gets him in the python hold with his elastic band arms and pushes him off, "fair enough then kid am off for another joint an a brandy then am gona watch apocalypse now, I might even watch it in that cini down stairs mush, see ye later", and with that H was off to his room and Dave was free to enjoy his night. The boys Brian and Blade are doing their katas, they're each going through a varied mix of different martial arts; Brian's going to do his for an hour or so and then its joint bevy and DVD, he picked up Sin City, he fuckin loves it, it's one of his favourite films (it's a wonder the sad cunt isn't watching a Wolverine movie, but he's seen them all so many of times, so it's a bit of Sin City for Bri) Blade on the other hand is just getting warmed up he's going to do his katas for a bit and then he's going down to the gym for a few hours, he doesn't sleep to well and never has, so he usually trains or does some free running through the night, but as soon as he saw the gym and Brian's training horse, plus all the other equipment he couldn't wait to jump in, so that's his night sorted out. The girls Mel and Lysa are being a bit boring tonight, although, it has been a long and stressful day, they've both settled down with a glass of their favourite respected tipple, and also rolled themselves a nice joint of whatever weed they brought with them. Lysa has brought up the matrix trilogy to watch but she'll probably only be able to get through one, and Mel is watching human traffic, the old rave movie set in Wales with John Simm and Danny Dyer, she's on her second bevy and third joint so she's laughing her head off because the movie is fucking hilarious. Brodi, on the other hand couldn't get over the games room, fucking dynamite, and so he's back down there, he's had a few goes of the video games and then he's going to have a few games of pool with himself, then it's off to the cinema to watch the Blu-ray of Riding Giants, he found it before in the library and couldn't believe it, it's Stacey Peralta's documentary film about the birth of big wave surfing, he fuckin loves this movie, he constantly fights with himself about which is the best Stacy movie, but he thinks Riding Giants might just be out in front, probably because he knows most of the lads in the movie, he's surfed with Laird Hamilton and Gerry Lopez loads of times, and because he's so old he even surfed with some of the old great pioneers like Mickey Munoz and the greatest most daring of them all, Greg Noll (da Bull), he hasn't seen Greg in years, and he's gutted because he used to love the guy, he was a great fuckin laugh, but he's scared to see anyone from that long ago, given to the fact that he doesn't age, so after a good few years he tends to stay away from people he's gotten to know. So, most of the guys nights are sorted out all except Sid and Emma. Sid, is not in his room? Emma, is in her room, she picked a great room with a massive walk in closet, just like the one she has at home, it took her a while to get everything unpacked and hung up, drawers filled, and perfumes and girly stuff all put out on her vanity table. She got some great DVD's from downstairs, a couple of movies, Sex in the City and Ten things I hate about you, a couple of great girly movies for a top girly, that's what she thought when she picked them out, she also got a couple of workout DVD's, Zumba the crazy Latin dance workout, and the Ministry of Sound pump it up for a little fun workout. She's going to watch a girly movie, have a nice Jack Daniels and smoke a nice joint, but not until she's done her workout, then she'll be fucked and in the mood. The ministry of sound is on pretty loud, she's doing her workout and has been for the last half hour; she's nearly finished. She's only got back stretches and leg stretches left to do, she's got her lovely long blond locks tied up in a bun so it doesn't get in the way. She's on all fours pushing her back down and lifting her head as high as she can stretching her back, she stands up to do the last of her leg stretches. She's got on her white training leggings, they're skin tight and show every curve and muscle of her ass and beautiful toned legs, they actually look sprayed on to be fair, her leggings that is, and there's sweat in all the right places. Her top is just a loose fitted belly top, her legs are slightly spread, she's bending over touching her toes, her top just slightly exposing those luscious breasts. Then as she slowly comes back up she arches her back with her arms held straight out, she's done about forty-six and is on the last four when she hears a weird moan, at the same time she feels something wet hitting her back and ass, she knows what's happened immediately and spins, as she spins she throws out the hardest kick she's ever done. You may have forgotten that earlier on that I said Sid was not in his room, that's because he was in Emma's room, so let's put the story in reverse a little. Sid is standing behind Emma and has been for some time, his cock's in his hand and he's doing some frantic wanking. The cunts pulling the head off it like you've never seen, cracking one off that would put us all to shame. The workout DVD is on quite loud so Emma can't hear him, now, he didn't mean to blow his load, well, not actually on Emma, but as she started doing her last workout it just got too much for him to handle and he lost his composure, he forgot where he was, when Emma bent over, her sweat soaked leggings sucked into her minge creating the most beautiful and pulsating camel toe he'd ever seen, that fat minge-doughnut was mouth-watering. At the same time her top was hanging loose and her huge braless-sweat-covered-breasts were doing an upside-down show for him, and that's when it all went wrong, he lost control and before he knew it he was shooting his load, unfortunately for Emma it was all over her. Fast forward now to a guttural scream and that would be Sid getting kicked in the hard on, it's bad enough getting kicked between the legs but when you've got a hard on and just that second blew your load it's about a million times worse. Emma knows she hit the fucker right in the bull's-eye, she doesn't use her telepathic powers, instead she uses the rare diamond head butt, she turns her head into a rock-hard diamond and gives Sid a head but he'll never forget, "You dirty little bastard" says Emma as her head turns back to its natural form, Sid is lying on the floor with his pants around his ankles, he's holding his balls with one hand and his head with the other.

H has rolled himself a few joints, he's got a good selection of different weed's, he's built a lemon haze, laughing buddha, diesel, and a nice scuff joint, he's poured himself a brandy and is contemplating a movie in bed or in the cini. He decides on the cini because as H is, the fucker can't keep still, or more to the point he's always got to have somebody to talk too. H is trudging down to the cini as Sid staggers past holding his head and balls and looks to H like he's had a good pasting, "you all right kid" asks H, Sid doesn't even acknowledge H he just falls into his room. Fucks up with that cunt, thinks H as he bounds down the stairs into the library. H has Apocalypse now but decides to have another look through the library, he's fucking dancing as he finds Dog town and Z boys, the skating documentary by Stacey Peralta, fuck it, I'm watching this he's thinking as he moves into the cini room, but then he hears the distinct sound that all men love, (pool balls clacking off each other) so he's off to investigate. He finds Brodi in the games room playing pool by himself, "now then mush ye playin by yeself I'll av yer a game if ye want" says H as he swans in. Brodi looks up at H smiling and then he sees the DVD H is holding. At exactly the same moment H puts his brandy joints and DVD on a table and clock's Brodi's DVD he brought in for later, the two of them look up at each other with massive cheesy grins. Joints are sparked, pool balls are set up, and drinks are poured as the two kindred spirits set themselves up for a whopper of a night. And sadly, that's how are first night at the manor comes to a close.

Everywhere 2009.

If H was to put into words how Superman was feeling his lovely scouse accent would be saying, "me fuckin eds burnt out mate" but it's not H, it's superman with no accent at all, so it's more like "I am mightily confused", he did everything he always does when he goes out, he finds a tramp and give him some money for his flashers coat so he can hide his superman suit. He then went to all the houses and places where he last saw the Marvellous but there was nobody to be found, it was as if they had disappeared of the face of the planet. He went to Liverpool first to see Mr Fantastic and the Hulk but there was nobody home, and now he's just finished knocking at the Sandman's home in Newquay, he wasn't home either, so he fly's up to the roof and tries to sort out his frazzled brain. He's so confused and scared and he feels ashamed, he's beating himself up again, calling himself a weakling "I'm a shadow of my former self" he tries to make himself man up, going over what he did at the houses "why am I so weak, all I did was knock on the door I didn't even use my x ray vision, I could have done anything, ripped the door from its hinges, burnt the lock with my laser eyes" but now he's thinking like a weak fool again "I didn't want to break my friends door down though." So, he decides on the first of his thoughts "I will try it out here first" he looks at the roof of the building and tries to remember how to use his x ray vision when POW, a vision pops on to the roof, there's a man and a woman going at it doggy style on a bed, Superman looks away immediately feeling embarrassed, "well I never" says Superman, he had completely forgot how clear his x ray vision was, he's also a little confused. How were this sweet loving human couple who were obviously trying to make a baby going to do this when the man was pushing his mating organ into the woman's anus, this isn't the way you conceive a child thought Superman, he carried on debating over this point as he glides down to the Sand man's apartment. He lands on the balcony and looks through the window, he scans the room and zooms in on the items he thinks are important, calendars, books, post it notes on the fridge, finally he spies some letters on a table and starts to x ray scan them, but there's nothing. Superman turns and looks over the sea wondering what he should do next, I will go to

Emma frost's house, it is the closest abode from here and the Invisible man lives nearby also, it will kill two birds with one stone. Superman shoots into the sky so fast not even a radar could pick him up, he's getting the hang of this flying lark, he sets his sonar navigator on Emma frost's apartment balcony and Woooosh. He lands on the balcony seconds later in total neo style, kind of half crouched with his arms slightly held out for effect, he raises his huge frame and walks to the window and begins the same routine as he did at the Sandman's. This balcony is different though, it doesn't look into the sitting room it looks into her bedroom, Superman scans the room but all he can see is some perfumes, clothes and girly ornaments. He's just about to leave when he notices a key card for a door scanner but there's nothing written on it, its sitting on an envelope, he super scan's the envelope and there's a letter, he super scan's the letter, it takes him a while because he's reading backward and upside down but eventually there it is, an address.

The Cave 2009.

This is fantastic, this is my ultimate dream, and I am in heaven. These are the thoughts of Magneto as he wobbles of to bed with tears streaming down his face, he doesn't usually have to go to bed but it's been a long emotional tiring night and he's fucked. Spiderman went to bed hours ago and missed the best of the show (fuckin lightweight) and now only Sabretooth and Ra's al Ghul are left watching. On the screen in front of them the Invisible man is wobbling down the landing in severe pain holding his balls and his head and Sabretooth and Ra's al Ghul are in stitches, and just like Magneto there's also tears streaming down their faces, Magneto takes a last look back at his two friends and then carries on to his room, he's now lying in his bed finishing a joint and thinking of what he has just seen. These people are a joke, they have become more human than humans are, they are obsessed with their petty lives, what car do I drive, what aftershave do I put on, what clothes do I wear, yes Magneto is delighted, they haven't even used their powers except for petty show, it is as though they have forgotten that they have them, the Hulk is so nice he could be a Buddhist and my new mind control drug will put an end to him anyway, and his mucker, as he calls him, Mr fantastic, has done fuckall, in fact there's only one who has shown any skills at all, and that's because she was getting jizzed on by a sex beast, the only thing he uses his invisibility for is to spy on women, what a joke. I am even contemplating not even asking them to join our mission, they are too lightweight, I might just destroy them, yes, destroy them. Magneto takes a final toke on his bum nut of a joint, closes his eyes and for the first time in a very long time slips into sleep with a nice big smile on his face.

The Manor 2009 the next day.

It's quite early but most of the guys are up, Dave is in the kitchen he's crouched down in a ball holding is ribs, there's tears running down his face as he tries to control his fits of laughter, Emma is also in the kitchen as you may have guessed, she's telling the lads what happened last night, Dave looks up at Emma and waves his hand in mock apology, he finally controls himself enough to get some words out, "am sorry Emma but you've got to admit, it's fuckin hilarious, I think, an I'm being honest here, if I could turn invisible I'd of done the same thing girl, you are fuckin fit as fuck ye no, an we've all changed ye no, from back then", Emma looks at Dave with a cheeky grin on her face, " I must admit Dave I had a right laugh when he went limpin out me room, the dirty little bastard", Dave's fits of laughter erupt again, H is brewing some coffee, he's not laughing though, he's looking at Dave and Emma, his eyebrows are pinched together and there's a pretty serious look on his face, "fuckin out of order if ye ask me like, fuckin beastin a girl on the first night ere, he wasn't even pissed or anythink, he needs a fuckin dig if ye ask me", he points at Dave, "that could av been your sister or anythink", Dave starts pissing himself even more, "you always say that you fuckin loon an av told ye, I avnt got a sister" they both start pissing themselves at their little in joke. "No, come on seriously, continues H, your only stickin up for him cos yer a fuckin beast as well", Dave looks at H acting like he's just stabbed him, "out, ov, order, that kid, out of order, now shut up an get the coffee goin you've been doin it for fuckin yonks", "yer whatever dickedd" retorts H, Brian and Lysa are also in the kitchen and as H starts pouring the coffee he turns his attention on them, "wha do you's think then guys, do you's think he's a beast or wha", "arr fer fuck sake H" says Lysa "loosen up will ye it wiz only a little wank, an as ye mate says, she is fit as fuck, if I was a bloke ad fuckin wani fuck her", Emma goes all red and shy but she's really fuckin well chuffed, H is also red in the face and is glad of the support when Brian voices his opinion, "am oon the fence like to be honest ya no, cos like he is a bit of a beast like, cumin on ye leg an all" Dave can't help himself at this point and goes for it again with another fit of hysterical laughter at the thought of Sid's manwack hitting her on the leg and ass, H turns round from the coffee and shouts over Dave's laughter, "there ye go, Bri knows wha he's talkin about the fuckin fellas a beast, like I fuckin said you's are all fuckin twisted, there's only me and Bri who are normal", Brian continues, "but ye noo like H man, she iz fit as fuck like, even you was clockin her ass yesterday when she was coming in", H gives Brian the look of thunder as he turns back to the coffee, he's fuckin beetroot now and thinking he could fuckin kill that Brian the stupid twat, he thought he was sticking up for him and he goes and tells the girl something like that. Lysa is a little bit gutted that H was clocking Emma's ass and wonders if he was also clocking her ass also, but not to worry she's decided that tonight's the night anyhow, she's going to fuck his brains out. H puts all the mugs on the huge kitchen table and they all grab greedily at the good morning coffee, probably the best one of the day, "ye wont fuckin believe this, says H, but this coffee is that fuckin copy, fuckin, luwak", he says it like Jack Nicolson in the bucket list, "ye no the one that's made of shit", they've all had it before so to the annoyance of H nobody's surprised, and a collective bout of telepathy goes around as they all take a sip and say at the same time, "this is gooooood shit", "fuck you then ye gang o cunts" says H "you can make ye own fuckin coffee from now on", they all give H the puppy dog eyes, "come on big fella were only jokin" says Dave, H lightens up a little but he's one of those people that can't sit still so he's back up and asking who wants toast, "av ad a good look in the big freezers the smornin and there's loads of homemade bread so am doin doorstoppers, who fuckin wants some?" "Ooo yes please" go the shouts from everyone. So as H starts to make the toast, Brian whom has got a infatuated man crush with Dave and H, can't help quizzing them a little, "so lads come on then tell us wha yev been up to like, in all them years an all, av yiz always lived in the pool like", H is at the worktop and Dave as usual is sitting on his ass at the table, they start their little double act of telling the story between them and bouncing off one another. "Well", starts H, "yes and no kid, we've always lived in Liverpool but we've travelled round an that, ye know, we've been everywhere avn't we kid", "yer mush" says Dave as he takes over, "probably like most ov you, the first seventy years where fuckin shit, everyone was livin in shit, an travellin around was a fuckin trip to hell and back, we didn't dare travel did we kid, and I had him as well didn't I" he nods at H who's still busy making toast, but you can tell he can hear and knows that Dave is talking about him as he nods at his back because his shoulders are jiggling a little as he has a little laugh to himself, so Dave continues, "we didn't do much in them days to be honest , mostly we went round and bought properties an that, but once the fifties kicked in mate that was it, we were fuckin livin it large lar," H turns round with a fuckin massive tray of doorstop toast steaming with butter, "her ye go gang, tuck in muckers" he says as he puts them on the table, he gives Dave (whom is still smiling and nodding at his own sweet memories) a nod of appreciation and continues, "we started goin everywhere kid, all the rag time dances an that, and Dave was still tryin to calm me down back then, yer the fifties was ok mate, but when the sixties and the seventies kicked in whooo, hooo, we went everywhere kid didn't we". H slides onto a stool and is sitting next to Dave now nudging him with his arm, "didn't we kid didn't we, every cunt we seen back then am fuckin tellin ye, we seen the Beatles, the stones, Hendrix, Bob Dylan, Janice Joplin, led zep, the who, pink Floyd, The Doors, fuckin everyone we seen" says H as he swings his hand in the air and jumps up getting excited, Dave puts a hand on H, "put a few more toast on kid their fuckin gorgeous", only to calm his mate a little, H gives Dave's hair a scuffle as he jumps up to start more toast. "No prooblemo mucka" he says, "ye want peanut butter on some ov thum", "too fuckin right we do kid, you betta fuckin believe it" says Dave, "OOOw ye, that sounds fuckin top banana that does H" says Mel as she comes in from the gym, "I fuckin love peanut butter" she says this as she plonks her sweet toned ass on a stool. Brodi comes next following Mel but he hasn't been to the gym, he's been in the cinema all night with H, he fell to sleep so H left him to it. He also plonks himself onto a stool ready for some coffee and toast just as Emma cutting back into H and Dave's story throws a bomb shell at them. "I used to go out with Jim Morrison for a bit in the sixties, only for a few weeks, but he was a good laugh", she says it nonchalantly and doesn't realise until she looks up that the whole room is silent and staring at her in amazement. "You, are, fuckin jokin me arnt ye" says H, "you used to go wid the lizard king, I can't fuckin believe it. Lysa as always with one thing on her mind gives Emma the eyebrows as she asks Emma "ay Emma he was supposed to have a massive cock, is it true"? Emma has a shy little blush, "yer it was alroight, I can't remember it much now to be honest, oy remember goin to the whisky a few times with him, met Jimmy Hendrix one night, Jim was fucked but still got on stage wiv I'm". As H starts to bend Emma's ear about Jim, Sid comes in with a fuckin big coggy on his noggin, everybody welcomes him in but he does look very sheepish. "Mornin Sidney me old mucka" says Dave. H, subtle as ever, is staring at Sid's head. "That is what you call a fuckin coggy mate, a fuckin coggy and a half that mate" laughs H, as he points to Sid's head, "looks like a fuckin apple kid all red and rosy". He's laughing his head off now feeling better about the situation as he leaves the table and lets Sid sit next to Dave, "I'll put more coffee on ay, does anyone want more toast or anythin" everyone else gives Sid little smiles and nods letting him know that we all make mistakes. Brodi and Mel can tell somethings happened by the mood and the fucking big coggy on Sid head, but decide to ask questions later. Dave breaks the ice as usual, "so errr wha are we up to later then peeps. H is still laughing and thinking to himself at Sid's head, fuckin some coggy that, cunt deserved it though, but I'll let the cunt off for now, he's ad a good kickin. H is restless as always and needs to get out for a bit, am goin that skate park I seen on the way down, me mucka will come with me, he's thinking this as he marches back to the table with more goodies. The gang are all laughing when H comes over, "guess wha Lysa suggested we do tonight kid" says Dave as H throws the goodies on the table "fuckin Garry Oke kid, your fuckin fave", H's eyes light up and the smile that spreads across his face couldn't get any bigger. "Arrr me fuckin fave, a fuckin love karaoke, me an Dave are the fuckn karaoke kings mate, and ye wana see me set up guys, it's the fuckn shit, fuckinell, it's a good job I brought it with me, right, am goin and startin to set it up, but err" H pauses and turns to Dave with a sheepish look "listen mush, do ye fancy comin the skate park wid me" he asks Dave, Dave gives a groan and looks at H with pleading eyes "arrr come on kid we've only just got ere yesterday" H gives Dave the puppy dog eyes and Dave gives them back, neither wanting to submit, its Brian that steps in to save the day for Dave, " al go with ye like H if ye wonni me to" H is fuckin chuffed, "arr nice one Bri lad I knew one of ye wouldn't let me down, listen then, am gona set the karaoke up for the night then get me shit together and we're off kid". H goes up to start bringing the equipment down for the setting up of the karaoke, "ay H, am goni give you a run fe ya money with the Karaoke" says Lysa with a little twinkle in her eye. Loads moor shouts from everyone get fired at H about him getting his ass kicked at the Karaoke later. Brian goes up to get dressed for his little outing with H, and Dave, delighted that he got out of a journey wants to know if anyone fancy s a game of pool to which Blade and Brodi are only too glad to oblige, "fuckin compo time" says Dave, as he does a little dance out of the kitchen. The girls all decide to have a pamper day after all the driving and unpacking yesterday, that's nails done de fluffed with the epilator, a nice dip in the pool, sauna, jacuzzi, steam room, then they're going to do each other's hair for the night, plus a lot of chatting about the past, their lives and let's not forget the boys.

The Cave 2009.

Magneto has woken slightly hazy, he lies in bed thinking about last night, his good mood evaporated he rises from bed his mood becoming darker by the second, too much brandy and weed he thinks as he walks to the monitor room. He glides in and is presented with Sabretooth and Ra al Ghur still in the same position as the night before, still smiling and laughing. The white mist sets into Magneto's brain and the red-hot anger begins to rise through his body, his jaw juts out, his teeth clench. Fucking pair of cunts he's thinking, is this all they have done all night, watch those cunt-twat Marvellous bastards messing around. He storms over to see if they have logged anything of significance down, no, not a thing, not one iota, Magneto explodes at the two of them, "IS THIS ALL YOU HAVE DONE ALL NIGHT, WHY DONT YOU GO JOIN THEM", he storms out the room and down to his basement room, (well not really a room, because its huge, about half the size of a football field) He enters onto a balcony looking down into the room. In the room there are about two hundred people, at or in various stages of distress. Over the course of the past six-month or so Magneto and the mob have been kidnapping various members of all governments from all around the world. (it's been in all the newspapers and on all the TV news stations but none of the Marvellous would know anything about it as none of them give a fuck about the news). Most of the people in the room are milling around and the rest are sitting down, but all wear shackles at the hands and feet. Magneto stands on the balcony surveying the humans, look at them, vile creatures, only interested in their own survival, fucking kill everything else, use everything else, fuck all maters but us, well I'll teach you, dirty human scum, once I have finished with you and the Marvellous all humans will die. As Magneto thinks this his blood boils higher and higher, he's still furious with the other two and it looks like the humans are going to be his outlet.

Carl Preston had a cool job, nice car, and a fit woman on his arm most nights, that was until about three months ago when one night he walked around a corner and into the fist of Sabretooth. It's not too bad in the basement, there's toilets and some showers and the food's not bad, but he just doesn't know why he's here, or for that matter what he's done to be here. Carl's been around everyone in this room and they're all in the same boat, nobody knows why they're here, nobody has a clue. Suddenly Carls handcuffs click open and float into the air. He looks around and everybody else's handcuffs are doing the same, the handcuffs start to melt, it looks like mercury floating in the air and Carl is mesmerised, he's never seen anything like it, it's so beautiful. Suddenly all the metal flows into one blob. On the other side of the room there's a huge square block of metal about eight feet square, it too begins to glide through the air and hover over people. Nobody looks scared of the humongous floating metal, they're more fascinated, it's like an amazing David Copperfield trick, and as it floats over Carl as he looks up in wondrous awe at the humongous lump of super smooth metal, that is absolutely amazing he's thinking as it comes crashing down squashing him to a tomatoey squished pulp.

Magneto is full of rage and its only getting worse, the handcuffs turning to liquid was cool so he expected them to be in awe, but he thought the humans would all run when he brought the cube out. Ha, they soon shit when I doped it on that gawking fool, look at him now just a bloody mush. Magneto was right, the scene below was utter chaos, it went from wonder and awe to smash, bang, swish, blood, guts, bone, excrement, stench. People were screaming and running but there was nowhere to run to. Magneto from his perch spots a big fatty, (he fucking hates fatty's) "I fucking hate fatty's" says Magneto as he lifts the huge metal block, the fat man was spellbound in shock and his face pouring with tears, he was staring at the dead man's body or more to the point, the bits of twisted body hanging out of the sides. The cube is suddenly lifted up, it begins to hover toward the fat man, he panics and tries to run, but Magneto is on him in seconds and BLAM the fat man is mush. The room erupts into more frantic screaming as Magneto picks up the pace, BLAM, BLAM, BLAM, he's popping humans like crazy, trying to go for groups or good runners who can dodge, BLAM, BLAM, BLAM. Magneto works his way through about a quarter of the humans in the room before he gets bored with the cube.

Keeley Jones has thrown her guts up three times and pissed her pants twice, her face is smeared in snot and tears, that fucking thing missed me by inches she's thinking as she scrambles away once more, suddenly the cube stops and as before it starts to transform, first it turns from a square into a ball, a huge eight foot-ball and just as quickly the ball splits and splits and splits, soon there are hundred's getting smaller and smaller then thousands until they are about a half inch in diameter. Keeley looks around the room and everybody has stopped running they're still whimpering and crying, and now, instead of looking at the orbs in wonder it's sheer terror, for the poor souls know what's coming next. A man standing about ten feet away from Keeley is the first to go and she gets a birds-eye view, PING, right through his kneecap and PING, straight through the other, as the man falls PING, another straight through the brain. Keeley stands in shock but acutely aware that there are thousands of these balls suspended above her head as the room turns to utter pandemonium again. Keeley looks up at the thousands of balls above her, she sees Magneto standing on the balcony and stares straight into his eyes as another man gets sprayed with them. Keeley watches as all the balls rise up and form a twirling swirling cloud at the top of the room, the tiny metal balls start to twirl together slowly at first but then the cloud gathers speed, Keeley looks on in horror as a small tornado pops down from the cloud. The balls swoop down and touch the floor gathering in speed and width. Keeley feels hot liquid running down her legs as she lets out her last scream and the tornado of metal ball bearings turn her to soup.

Magneto is finished playing, he's furious and wants done, he touches the tornado down and goes straight for the hard case bird that was trying to stare him out, MUSH right through her, he then sends the tornado around the room at such speed that it's a horror bath, just blood, guts, bones, shit, piss and hair. He turns and walks from the room and back upstairs, as he ascends Ra's al Ghul and Sabretooth come down to meet him, maybe cheer him up but the look he gives them is ice cold, "go clean that fucking mess up" he says as he storms away. Ra's al Ghul gives Sabretooth a worried look, turns and runs down the stairs. When he reaches the bottom, the smell is the first thing to reach his senses and he retches before he's even in the room, he's terrified and doesn't want to look in, Sabretooth walks past him into the room, a moan escapes his mouth and Ra's al Ghul steps through, he stands looking at the devastation as tears start to stream down his face.

The Skate park 2009.

Brian is sitting in the spectator zone, it's a balcony that overlooks the skate park where you can get refreshments and such. H is on his board doing his stuff, and to the astonishment of Brian he's pretty fucking good, in fact he's shit hot. Brian, is just starting to calm down after the drive over where he let H take the wheel of his Aston Martin DBS, (he never knew the car could do such things). H is fucking loving it here, it's one of the best skate parks he's ever been to, there's some really good clear long runs if you want to carve the fucker up, but the real joy is the ramps and bowl's, this fucker has half pipes, quarter pipes, spine transfers, handrails, full pipes, snake runs, fun boxes, vert ramps, the fucking lot. There's not many people at the park today and it's so big you probably wouldn't notice if there was, H doesn't give a fuck though he's having the time of his life, he's got his earphones in, his music's blasting and he's flying. There's a small gang of teenagers sitting along one of the walls watching H do his stuff and as I said H is pretty good, he's been skating round for a while now and hasn't made that many fuck-ups. Brian has been well impressed, he's on the balcony leaning over watching H and doing ooo's and arrr's every time H pulls off a top trick. H is lost in his music, he's listening to Radio Head's version of Wish you were here, its beautiful piano accompanied by that weird backwards music shit like the song from the Coocoo's nest that fuck me, sounds so good. He's carving around one of the bowls, he straightens out and dips into the bowl and whoooosh, H flies up, knocks out a three sixty and boooom he's back flying through the bowl. The next song comes on and it's Pharrell and Gwen singing Can I have it like that, the hypnotic base hits H straight away, Boom BBBBBB Boom BBBBBB, then Pharrell comes in, "Yo, on and on my nut's, I'm palming, take two of these and call me in the morning". H's head is bobbing as he carves the huge bowl again, he goes past the boys and notices that they're watching him, H gets a little bit confident and decides to show boat, he flies to the end of the bowl, pulls a quick one eighty and uses all his frontside force to get speed, as he cruises past the lads he does that thing all dickheads do with earphones on, he thinks they can hear the song and also that he's not singing so loud, the stupid cunt doesn't realise that all that the kids can see is a mad old fella flying past nodding his head shouting "CAUSE MY NAME IS SKATE.......BOARD........P". Brian's upstairs laughing his head off at H's sudden outburst of song. H straightens out to pull off his big move, he's flying through the bowl, as he approaches the end he knows what he's going to do, he flies out of the bowl into the air, and that's where it all goes wrong, he flips up the wrong way, "OO SHIT" gasps H, his board is air Bourne and gone, H is upside down and heading for the deck with speed, SSSLLLAAAMMM, H's face hits the ramp and EEEEEEEEEECH, screeches down it with that sound that's almost as bad as nails on a chalk board. "FFFUUUCCCKKK" is the long drawn out word that escapes H's lips as he comes to a halt. Brian, and the lads erupt into peals of laughter, but that only lasts for a split second for Brian is quickly shut up and nearly shits his pants as H's head snaps up and looks at him with the brightest green eyes. Brian quickly turns the colour of boiled shite, O fuck he's goni change like, thinks Brian, he's just about to vault over the balcony and try to calm H down when H breaks into a huge smile and starts to laugh his head off, the lads on the side begin giving H a round of applause, he's got a massive burn mark running down his cheek but luckily it's already healing, you can see that it will soon be gone, Brian starts to laugh again as H slumps down and gives Brian and the lads a fuck you finger each.

The Manor 2009 Karaoke night

Its early evening time at the manor house and everybody's in the kitchen cooking dinner and snacks for the coming night and party. Everybody's suited and booted and looking fresh as fuck, even Sid's had a shower and looks dapper. H has done a fantastic job in the communal room; the main area of the room is sunken to the rest so H has set the Karaoke machine up on the higher level so it looks like whomever is singing is on a stage. He's arranged the wraparound sofa at the other end for maximum viewing pleasure and placed the huge table in front of the couch with everybody's favourite tipple on it. There's all kinds, Whiskey, Brandy, Jack Daniels, Southern Comfort, Vodka, Malabo, Gin, wine, Rum, Baileys, port, and loads of shot bevvy like Tequila, Sambuca, Jägermeister, and loads of mixers like, Schnapps, Tonic water, Lemon and Lime and all that shit, the table looks fucking boss. H has also set up a weed table and asked everybody for some weed so he gets a good mixture, there's some Moroccan, Jamaican, Pollen, Scuff, Blonde and some top Skunk,

White widow, Laughing buddha, Super Lemon haze, Blue cheese, Vanilla Kush and some SS haze. The gang have only cooked some light Italian for the meal as they've done loads of snacks for later. They're just finishing up and H has scooted off for some last-minute tweaking, his laptop's all hooked up and the list of hits on his Karaoke program is the shit, there's not a song that's not on it. The gang are all laughing and in good spirits as Brian has just finished telling them the tale of the skate park, Dave's in pleats of laughter and telling one of his own "so we go to the pictures right, to see that Guy Richie movie Snatch yer, an we're at this kiosk gettin loads o stuff, I just love them big buckets ov popcorn an a fuckin big barrel bevvy ov coke" everyone's fixed to Dave nodding and laughing thinking mmmmm yes me too as Dave goes on. "But this (he prods his finger at the kitchen door to where H is outside) fucken fussy cunt H wants fuckin hot dogs an all that shite, so I'm standin with me stuff waitin for H an there's a lad an his bird standin behind H in the que an she's fit as fuck, little blond number, so H is standin lookin at the lad behind the counter an the lads lookin at H, an H is fuckin all wound up cos the lad hasn't give him any condiments, so H kind of growls at the lad, where are theeey, an the lads all lost an shitin himself cos he can see H is getting all wound up, an he says to H "all what mate" now soft cunt here's fuckin fumin and he's shoutin, the fuckin condiments lad, the fuckin condiments, tomarta sauce an that" the whole room again are laughing, because they know what Hulk is like when he's getting wound up "so the lad points right next to H, they're there mate, and ye know what he's like, fuckin big smile breaks out cos he's been a dozy cunt, nice one lad he says to the kid who starts to serve the lad an his fit bird, so H picks up the tomarta sauce an his hot dog's on the counter on a little serviette, he goes to squeeze some on an the lid right, the lid fuckin fly's off and the whole fuckin bottle of sauce goes FUCKIN SPLOOSH all over the hot dog, fuckin all over H, fuckin all over the floor, an fuckin all over the poor lad an his fit bird, there was even some on me but am fuckin pissin myself, nearly dropped me fucking popcorn, swear to god I was cryin it was fuckin hilarious, H is fuckin fumin, he turns to me an I can see his eyes goin green, but to be fair to the cunt when he spots me fuckin cryin wid laughter a fuckin big smile breaks out, but as he turns back to the fuckin counter his hot dog right, cos its top heavy goes glup, glup, glup an fuckin rolls right across the counter like one of them beach balls from years ago with a bit of sand at the bottom, an that was me mate I nearly did piss myself". The gang are pissing themselves and asking Dave all kinds of questions about the guy behind the counter and the guy with the fit bird as H comes back in, he's right in the middle of taking a toke of a fucking humongous fat spliff, "you betta not be laughin at me ye gang o cunts" shouts H as he strolls to the table, "am just tellin them about the time we went to watch Snatch mate "says Dave. H starts laughing "arr wha a fuckin nightmare, fuckin tomarte sauce everywhere, took me fuckin ages to get cleaned up". H starts to put the dinner plates in the dishwasher and starts to order everyone about, you can tell he's getting excited, " Blade lad, do us a favour mate an take them snacks in an put them on the big table, Dave can you get the glasses ready kid, they're in that cupboard over there, we need shot glasses as well mush, Bri an Brodi come on lads make yeselves useful, get in there an get a few joints rolled, LETS GET THIS FUCKIN PARTY STARTED" shouts H as the girls all start whooping and screaming.

Outside the Manor 2009

Superman is standing outside the manor, he's been using his x ray vision to look through from a distance but it's not as good as up close. There's only been one person in the room that he's looking into and he thinks it's the Hulk, he can see him tinkering with computer devices and speakers and a massive plasma screen on the wall. Then after a while the Hulk sits down with a board on his knee and a jar of green plant like stuff and starts to make some kind of smoking contraption, when he's finished he lights the long fat white cigarette-looking contraption and goes out, and a few moments later the whole gang appear all laughing, and from the looks of it in great spirits, hhmmmm thinks Superman, they don't seem to be in any sign of trouble. Superman taps into the room with his super hearing and starts to listen. He's so engrossed by the scene playing out before him that as he watches the gang he's has been inching closer and closer to the window for a better look, the gang all look the same but they seem to have changed beyond all recognition also. He's now transfixed listening to the conversation, he's desperate to knock at the front door and go see his old buddy's, they seem to be having a great time together, but he's apprehensive because he knows he messed up all them years ago, all that badgering and moaning I did and I was the one to go ruin everything, I was the one to let the cat out of the bag. Superman doesn't know what to do he just knows they're going to go ballistic when they find out, they will disown me, the Hulk will probably rip me limb from limb. As Superman ponders the mistakes he's made he suddenly hears one of the girls scream and shout, "thar's a fuckin weird tramp lookin throo the windy", "o no, no, no" cries Superman waving his hands and walking backward as he watches the Hulk running for the front door shouting "FUCKIN...., DIRTY...., HOUSE ROBBIN TWAT, AL RIP THE FUCKIN CUNTS EDD OFF".

America New York 1958.

Stan Lee is pissed off, and he's bored, writing is his life, without it he may as well top himself, he loves writing, but the writing he's being told to do lately is killing him, it's so depressing. Stan sits nursing his beer pondering his life and wondering where it's going. His wife keeps telling him to be more adventurous, he has some good ideas but he needs to elaborate on them more, but Stan's not sure, it's only his wife that thinks that. Stan's been in the bar for a few hours and he's fairly drunk. The door to the bar suddenly fly's opens, Stan turns his head to the door and watches a huge man enter the bar. The man is wearing a long nasty looking and probably stinking of shit trench coat, Stan hears the barman yell at the man "HEY GET THE FUCK OUT PUNK ". The man reaches into his dirty coat and produces a bundle of notes "I have currency", he waves the notes in the air as he walks toward Stan, "is this stool taken my friend" he asks Stan, "errrr no, no, take a seat friend". The man sits down and orders three beers, he passes one to Stan, takes one of the others and downs it in one, he looks at Stan as he pulls his other beer close and starts to sip at it. Stan notices that the man already looks a bit worse for wear, his eyes are drowsy and Stan was right in his assumption that he does fucking stink. Stan for some reason unbeknown to him decides to lend a kind ear to the man as he seems so depressed, and Stan's worried he might do himself some harm. Stan orders two triple shots of his favourite whiskey, "here buddy, Stan hands the man the shot of whiskey "you look like you could do with a kind ear son, what's on yer mind". The man looks at Stan with tears brimming in his eyes, and so begins an all-night out-pour of his life. At first the man is only telling him of his depression and how he lives with his mother and father, and that of lately they have started to bully him constantly, "they call me shit house and cunt face, these are my parents" then he starts to tell of his old friends and how he misses them so, but as the night wears on and the drinks keep flowing he gets more and more loose with his tongue and his tales. Stan listens as best he can in his drunken stupor as the man starts to tell tales of immortality, and beings with extraordinary powers, fights of good and evil, truths and lies and pacts and promises. Stan and the man fall out of the bar in the early hours and as they stagger up the street Stan hails a cab and jumps in, he keeps the door open and offers the man a ride, but the man waves him off and staggers away. When Stan gets home he's elated, he has so much material there's no way he's sleeping, he can even share some of them with his friends. He tries with all his bearings to scribble all that he could remember about the night he'd just had and the stories and characters he heard of, he stays up for hours and hours but to be honest he probably got a bit muddled up, but that was definitely the end of Stan's depression.

Superman wakes in an alleyway the next day, he's dizzy, hazy and felling the effects of a hangover. He opens his eyes to a man rummaging through his coat. He grabs the man's hand and starts to crush his bones, the man is screaming, Superman lets him go, he looks into his eyes and says " go away", the man scuttles of down the alleyway as Superman clears his head of the hangover and starts to recall in detail the events of the night before, " ooo nooooo" he wails, Superman is trembling and his mind is swimming with panicked and paranoid thoughts, what have I done, what have I done, I have doomed us all, the others will kill me I have doomed them, they will be persecuted. He gets up and dusts himself down, he has a thought that he could just pay Stan a visit but he'd probably have to kill him, but the thought of harming a human being repulses him more than anything ever imaginable. He pushes the thought to the back of his mind and decides to go home, he springs to the top of the building he's standing next to and surveys the land and building to affirm that nobody is watching. Superman shoots into the air and heads home, as he glides through the sky his thoughts and fears of the night before fester, it turns into a deep paranoia and continue to do so for almost seventy years, he never leaves his palace again, that is until 2009.

The Cave 2009.

Spiderman is in his room. He's working on a new device for the master and he couldn't be happier. He's left the other two idiots to their own devices tonight, no snooping, spying, or eavesdropping, just pure mechanical bliss. As he work's you can see a huge smug grin on his face as he hums to the sounds of The Outsider, the song by a Perfect circle, he has the album Emotive on, the music melding with his nasty scheming mind. He's revelling in the bliss of his boss finding the other two fuckheads enjoying the show that those dirty-maggot Marvellous are putting on, and of what his Lordship then did to the disgusting hoard of human scum that dared litter our basement. He's definitely the gaffas numero uno now, the master was not happy with his once friend Ra al Ghul and his softness for the humans. And her, he hasn't mentioned for a long time, Spiderman knows the boss hasn't forgotten her but the longer she's gone the better for little Spidey. He grins as he fixes another part to the massive metal contraption, lost in his thoughts of how the master had only shared his new plans with him, "you alone I can trust Spiderman" were his last words before he left. Spiderman doesn't drink much, but tonight is different, so he's poured himself a nice glass of whiskey. He sits back in his chair and thinks about the glorious new truth, I am the bosses number one, and me alone does he trust completely.

Ra's al Ghul and Sabretooth have not long finished the cleaning of the massacre, and to be fair it wasn't that hard, there's a huge water cannon at one end of the room and a grate at the other, they just turned it on at let the machine do the work, but that isn't to say that it wasn't gross or horrific or traumatising, watching all that god knows what floating away. The worst bit was when they had to get in and get all that nasty shit off the walls. In their rooms they both sit contemplating the day they've had and wondering what the future will bring. They've been searching for the Marvellous for so long that now they have them it all seems so stupid, and the taking over the world shit they never really believed anyway, I mean, a hundred years ago it was a good idea, but now, in this day and age it's a bit far-fetched, and as I said, a bit fucking stupid. They've both showered and dressed and have just met at the screens, they know Spidey is in his room and will be all night, but they're not sure where Magneto is and to be honest they really don't give a fuck, not tonight, and not after the day they've had, and to top off a fucker of a day they find out when they hit the screens that the girls have had a pamper day, and also dolled themselves up for tonight. They've just found this out from the chatter on the screens, it's from the girls and there looking at each other shaking their heads "what a fucker my friend, I bet they've been walking round naked and in little thongs all day" says Ra's, Sabretooth laughs as he takes his first long swig of brandy, "ooooooo... yes, and showing and shaving each-others pussy's, and comparing tities" says Sabretooth, they're both pissing themselves, "O my, is that really what women do when they have a pamper day" asks Ra with a sly cheeky grin, "it is in my world" says Sabretooth as they both start howling. The boys have both brought a few bottles of their favourite tipple and a couple of shot tipples also, and of course the night wouldn't be right without a fine mound of super green, in fact, Ra's has just sparked a nice fat one, he leans back in his chair and takes a long hard drag sucking in the sweet purple smoke, as he exhales he takes a long swig of Jack. On the screens the gang are just finishing up dinner, chatting about the night ahead and moving on in to the main room. There's spliffs getting sparked and glasses getting filled. Ra's al Ghul and Sabretooth both turn at the same time and clink glasses, Ra's passes Sabretooth the joint and rests his hand on his shoulder, "I don't know what lies ahead for us my friend or even how long we have left ourselves, this crazy scheme is getting out of hand and the gaffa seems to have lost the plot wouldn't you say" Ra's laughs as he puts his drink down and takes the joint back from Sabretooth, Ra's carries on with his little speech patting Sabretooth on the shoulder, so tonight bro lets smoke, drink and sing ourselves into oblivion" " I like de fucken sound a dat" answers Sabretooth in his best Hulk impersonation, he lifts his glass to Ra's who is in stitches laughing. Ra's al Ghul reaches for his glass but as he does Sabretooth sits forward staring at the screen of the courtyard, "hello my friend, you little sneaky, sneaky and who would you be" he says this as he swipes the remote to zoom in. As they zoom in to get a better look at the stranger they see that he's so enthralled by what's happening in the manor he doesn't notice that he's inching closer and closer to the window of the manor, and just as they zoom to his face one of the girls on the screen screams and shouts "thars a fuckin weird tramp lookin throo the windy". As the madness unfolds on the screens Ra's al Ghul and Sabretooth both look at each other with wide grins, "as I said my friend" says Ra's "this is going to be one hell of a night".

The Building 2009.

"Magneto is in the building" shouts Magneto to absolutely nobody. Magneto is in a huge old building. The interior looks like it was once a nightclub with different levels everywhere and platforms where dancers once swung on poles, but now it looks like it's been empty for some time. There's a huge circular dance floor that sits below the entrance and Magneto stands in the middle with his arms raised, he's thinking of the days soon to come. My plan is coming to fruition, this is where it will happen, this is where the Marvellous will meet their end. He looks over to a podium on the right, this is where I will put Mr Fantastic's death device, he looks to the podium on the left, and this little space is for Superbollocs if he shows up, he looks to the main stage directly ahead, and this is where you Mr Hulk will cease to exist. Magneto settles himself in for the night and starts to build the contraptions that will hold the Marvellous, happy in his thoughts and to be out of the cave for a while.

The Manor 2009 Karaoke night continued.

The gang had just all walked into the room, plates were getting placed, drinks were getting filled, joints were being rolled and the banter was flowing good and proper, then BAM, Lysa spots a man in a fuck ugly trench coat looking through the window, "thars a fuckin weird tramp lookin throo the windy". H is closest to the door, he turns to it and shouts at the same time "FUCKIN...., DIRTY....., HOUSE ROBBIN TWAT, AL RIP THE FUCKIN CUNTS EDD OFF". H flies for the door and flings it open, he's outside in a flash. The gang are momentarily stunned and looking at one another, then in a collective bound they all spring for the door, but just as the gang reach the door, "RAAAA" H jumps into the door jam and, "WWAAAAAA" go the whole gang as they jump back, H is pissing himself as he walks in "ay, you'll never guess oos jonin us fe the party". H steps out of the way as the tramp walks through the door and raises his head. "WWWOOOOOO SUPERMAN" shout the gang as they go in for group hugs and back slaps and handshakes, but they soon back off when they see the nasty trench coat, "wha the fucks that Soop" says Dave pointing at the foul coat, "e arr kid giz that filthy fuckin stinkin rag an I'll bin it". Superman takes off his coat and hands it over to Dave. Now there it is, The Suit, all fresh and sparkling, now the gang all go in for the hugs. Superman is overwhelmed and almost starts to blubber but holds it in as he's dragged into the main room. The gang are all telling Superman their names, and where they've been living, and what they've been up to, then Superman gets a glass of Whisky in the hand and then gets a grilling on where he's been and what he's been getting up to. Superman skirts around most of it, "did you bring us all here kid, is this your house" says H as he waves his hand at the manor in general, "no I did not my friend, I... I had a strange feeling and I knew I just had to find you", "how did ye find us kid" asks Dave, "I have always known where you are, all of you, but I have never visited you I just knew where you lived", "yer but how did yow find us here thow" asks Blade, "arrr yes, I saw a key card and a note in err... Emma is it ", Emma nods and blushes at the same time, "yes in Emma's apartment a...a...a", Superman stutters and looks at Emma again, "only through the window though miss Frost, I wouldn't dare enter your apartment". The gang all burst out laughing at Superman's last remark, "yer a fuckin whopper you Soop" says H, but then H's face sets all serious, he points his finger at Superman, "ye didn't sniff her knickers did ye Soop, did you go inter her bedroom an sniff her knickers ye dirty bastard you" Superman's face is beaming. his heads twitching and his hands are flapping in front of himself as he's shouting, "no... no..no". H bursts out laughing as does everyone else and he grabs Superman in a little matey headlock, "am only fuckin with ye Soop lad, just a bit O banter ay kid", says H. Superman takes a huge swig of his drink as H lets him go. H sits forward and scans the gang for a joint, "who's gora joint for our Soop here mushes", "hear ya goo man" says Brian as he passes Superman a nice fat cone, "rolled to perfection by Dave that woos", Superman takes the joint and looks at the gang raising his eyebrows, "its awright Soop" says Mel "it'll calm your nerves boyo, youw look a bit flustered youw do". Superman takes a long hard toke on the joint, he takes the smoke down deep into his lung and lets his head fall back as he exhales, "pphhhhhhhhhh". Superman's brings his head back down and looks around the gang, "yes... a nice calming effect, I think I like it". The gang are all laughing and giving superman the high fives and it sets the mood in motion, everyone starts chatting, building joints, pouring drinks, the nights going to be a good one. Now that Superman has had a bit of Whisky and a toke of a joint he starts to revert into himself again, he knows H is talking to him but he's only half listening because he can't stop thinking about Stan Lee and the blunder he made, especially because the gang have been so nice to him. He's also confused as to who has asked them all to come to this place and how they, whomever it is, knew where they lived. He hears H saying something about Karaoke and being first on the mic, he starts to panic a little, he knows he must tell them the truth about the dangers he has put them in whatever the consequences. H stands up and turns to head for the laptop and mic," WAIT" says Superman, H turns back and looks down at Superman as do all the gang, Superman bows his head a little, afraid and ashamed to look at them" I have something to tell you all, I do not know who sent you those letters and asked you to come here and it is all very puzzling, and I do not think we should take this lightly, we have no idea whom this could be, but... but", Superman stammers, he sits forward and puts his face in his hands, " I have something horrid to confess to, I am ashamed of myself", H comes over and sits next to Superman, he puts his arm around him, "e arr Soop kid, what's up mush, it's alright mush, yer aint done nottn to us kid", says H, superman shakes his head, "I have lied and hidden myself from you, I knew where you were but I was so ashamed of what I had done that I could not come and see you, not even to warn you". The gang are all raised eyebrows, looking at each other with quizzical glances. "It was me" says Superman "it was me who told Stan Lee about us all, me who put us all in so much danger, me.... I am the idiot". Superman's head is still in his hands and the gang are all gasping looking at each other in surprise and astonishment. "Wait a minute kid" says H, he takes his arm away from Superman and turns slightly to face him "but you was the one who told us to split up an that, so no one would find out about us", H is wagging his finger at Superman as he talks, "so how did you end up being the one te tell everyone about us". Superman looks up at H and then around at all the faces, he sits back and takes a deep breath, he looks at the joint in his hand turning it, he places the joint in his mouth and puts a lighter to it, takes a massive toke, he keeps the smoke in his lungs for a moment and then phhhhhhh. The gang are getting more and more excited by the second but also a little bit anxious because H seemed a little pissed off at Superman. Superman looks at H "I am sorry my friend, it was a long time ago.... I was very, very depressed". Superman goes on to tell the gang about the night in nineteen fifty-eight, his meeting with Stan and of what ensued. As superman comes to the end of his story he's looking at H and his eyes are filling up, "I'm so, so, sorry my friends ". H is shaking his head looking at Superman and then round at all the gang, "is tha it" says H, "is tha all ye was worried about, Fuckin tellin Stan Lee about us, are you avin a fuckin laugh ye soft cunt". H grabs Superman in a huge bear hug. "cum here ye big soft cunt ye". H is hugging Superman and the gang are all laughing a little, but in a consoling way, "look at all these kid" says H as he gestures to the gang, "do ye think these give a fuck about you tellin Stan, they're fuckin lovin it, the fuckin revelling in it, look at Brian there with his Wolverine sidys, or Blade there all in black, we fuckin love are comic book selves". Superman's looking at H with mild suspicion, he looks to the gang but they're all in the same boat as H, there's lots of back slapping and hugging. Blade comes in for a man hug "fuckinell Soop mate yow should ov just told us mate, we don't give a fuck". Next its all the girls in for hugs and soon Superman's laughing just glad of the reaction from the pack. The drinks are getting filled again and everyone's chatting and chilling. H suddenly remembers what the night's all about, he jumps up and gestures to Superman, "oor right muderfuckers lets show this cunt wha he's been missin. H strides to the stage, he presses a few keys on the laptop and a wall of sound hits the gang like a fucking sonic boom, it's the gritty sounds of a guitar from the Stooges Down on the street. Dave's shaking his head laughing "he always starts with dis, I can read him like a fuckin book", the gang are all laughing but delighted at H's choice of an opener. The intro guitars are crunching and H is taking no prisoners with his performance' he's screaming like Iggy "Wooooo...Woooooo.....Down on the street where the faces shiiiiiiiiin". The gang are ecstatic, screaming and whopping as H pulls off a classic. Brian's up next but he plays it safe with a golden oldie, I say he plays it safe but he pulls off Billy Fury's Wondrous Place with nothing but class, easing the gang into a nice comfort zone. H is pulling the he's not too bad face at Dave and Dave's nodding back. The girls are loving it, they're all up doing little mock Pulp Fiction dances. Brian jumps down from the makeshift stage and Mel swoops to the mic, "arrrr you bitch" scream's Lysa, Mel's laughing at Lysa as she scans the screen for a good song, her eyes light up as she spot's the one, she clicks the laptop and a beautiful guitar riff fills the room with sound. Dave's up as soon as he hears the riff, "I knew it... I knew you liked her" shout's Dave pointing at Mel, (earlier Dave had mentioned to Mel that she looked like Skin from Skunk Anansie and she'd brushed him off saying she didn't even know who she was), Mel's laughing her head off at Dave and pulling tongues at him, she almost misses her que. She grabs the mic, her head down and slithers into the roll, "I called you brazen, called you whore right to your face". Dave grabs H in a headlock he's so hyped up "I fucken LOVE dis song kid" shouts Dave, then he turns to Mel so he can join her for the chorus, "why don't you weeeeeep when I hurt you, why don't you weeeeeep when I cut you". Sid's sitting next to Brian asks "oooz that

song by then mate", "ow eeeer.... it's Brazen by Skunk Anansie Sid"
Sid's nodding "oy remember now, oy used to like dem, she's fuckin
good mate init" says Sid nodding toward Mel, Brian's nodding as Mel
finishes and comes down, as the girls are giving her a that was great
cuddle, Sid the sneaky fucker has gone invisible, he reappears on
stage too shouts from the gang of "you sneaky fucker", he's laughing
as he scans the playlist and also delighted that Brian pulled an oldie
off, he didn't want to be the first, he spots his tune and punches it in.
Blade's the first to react to Sid's choice when he hears the opening
bars, his eyebrows are raised and he's looking round the room at the
others in astonishment, its Solomon Burk's Cry to me, and no easy
song, but when Sid pop's his first line in Blade is up whooping,
"gooow on Sid". The gang can't believe it, for a little fella, Sid has a
massive voice. The girls are bopping close to Sid and get some of the
boys up for a little dirty dancing, (well.... you've got to when
Solomon's on). Dave plonks himself down next to Superman, he
throws his arm around him, "how ye dooin Soop kid" says Dave giving
Superman a little hug, "are ye gona have a go then Soop" asks Dave,
Superman looks at Dave a little confused "have a go at what my
friend?" "the fuckin Garry Oky" says Dave nodding toward the stage,
"Oooooo! the Karaoke, no. no...no my friend not tonight no" "why
not mate you'll fucken love it kid, tellin ye" "no...no, thank you
though Dave but tonight I think I will just watch". Dave gives
Superman the yer we'll see about that face as he pulls a fucking
massive blue peter here's one I made earlier joint from his pocket, he
pops it into his mouth and sparks the bad boy, he takes a few long
hard drags and flops back blowing smoke into the air. Sid has just
finished singing and before he even has the chance to pop the mic
back in its stand Lysa snatches it off him and is scanning the playlist.
Sid comes off the makeshift stage to back slaps and high fives and
plops himself next to Superman and Dave, but Lysa's choice booms

from the speakers and Dave's up whooping, he turns to the boys and passes his joint "err ye go boys am off", he bounces over to his mucka H to the sound of Annie Lennox's Little Bird and they're both raving and reminiscing, doing funny dances they used to do at the clubs. Superman passes Sid the joint that Dave passed them and Sid takes a long drag, he looks around the room at the gang and a huge grin spreads across his face. He loves the gang and can't believe how much, and how much he's missed them until tonight, he knows he's stoned and drunk but he'd been stoned and drunk in the past and never felt like this, this is different, after what he'd done last night and how the gang had treated him, they still loved him, they still wanted him around, Sid couldn't believe it. The gang had brought Sid out of his reclusive stupor and Sid was beating himself up for being the man he had been for so long, he vows to himself the minute he gets home he's going to destroy all the filth he's collected over the years, all them poor, poor, girls he has on tape, he loves his gang and never wants to disappoint them again. Superman turns to Sid to converse but Sid has a stern look on his face "are you ok my friend? You look troubled" asks Superman, Sid shakes himself out of his self-loathing thoughts and looks at Superman, a huge grin spreads across Sid's face "sorry Soop I wus lost in me thoughts then, but to answer your question mate oy never felt betta in me life mate", he gives Superman a huge hug "it's good to fackin see ya Soop, I'm glad ya showed up mate". Lysa has just finished her song, she pop's the mic into the stand and turns to Emma thumbing at the mic as she exits the stage but Blades having none of that, he jumps into the air and pulls of a triple flip landing at the mic, he pops it out of is stand as he points at Emma laughing. Blade's at the playlist trying to choose a good one but there's so many, he doesn't know if he should go oldies, rock, rave, blues, O what to do, what to do. Blade's just about to start to panic when he spots the one, he punches in his choice and swaggers back to the mic stand to the haunting intro of Adamski's Killer. Mel's up at the front of the stage whooping as Blade throws out his opening line and the room goes wild, even Sid jumps up to do the two bottles dance. H spots Superman on the couch and plonks himself down with a tray of weed and all the necessary paraphernalia, as he starts to build a joint he decides that Superman cannot go the night without having a go on stage, H decides to play on Superman's emotions and thinks he knows just the right form of leverage to use, "are ye not avin a go then mate" asks H, "no my friend, I have been asked many times, but for tonight I think no, I am enjoying myself too much as a spectator my friend", H presses on "yer kid but there's nothin that bonds people more than karaoke, if you sing up there mate them cunts el love ye forever", H is pointing at the gang and leaves the last line to simmer in Superman's scull for a bit as he continues with his joint. H can tell he's got Superman thinking as he spy's him from the side of his eye, he can almost feel him churning the idea over in his brain, he decides to throw in another line "if ye fancy avin a go anyway mate av got the perfect song for ye, are ye good at memorising lyrics an that", Superman looks at H "I can memorise anything perfectly H" "well then kid if ye fancy it give us a nod ye" "ok H I will keep it in mind, thank you" "no problemo mush" says H as he swipes his tongue across the papers and glues his joint shut, he rips some thin card from the skin packet and pokes in his roach. Superman sits brooding about what H has just been saying and also giving serious thought to jumping up on stage, he's just about to ask H about the song he was talking about when Blade's song come's to its end and Emma jumps up to retrieve him of the mic. Blade comes off stage to the usual high fives and back slaps as Emma scans the playlist. It doesn't take Emma long to find her opener, she punches in her choice and the speakers once more burst forth with the sweet sweet sounds of Kate Nashe's piano. Emma has

chosen the song Foundations and as soon as the first notes boom out
the gang are going crazy. H has only just put lighter to spliff when he
hears the opening piano chords boom out, he jumps up joint in
mouth and grabs Superman by the hands and hauls him from the
couch "cum on kid, ye not sittin this one out". The gang go wild when
they see Superman join the dancefloor, he doesn't really know any
dance moves so decides to copy H whose doing some kind of crazy
hey yar dance like Andre, but to be honest he doesn't really pull it
off, (he's all shoulders you see). H being the gent, saves Superman's
dignity when he notices Superman's awkward moves by starting the
old Madness dance, which to be fair to H fits the song perfect. H
starts the moves and Daves's right on it, jumping in behind H with the
same moves, soon enough everyone's joined in so there's a full-on
Madness line all moving in unison. Emma on stage is finding it hard
not to laugh, and to add to it the songs not too easy to sing, but
nobody gives a fuck anyhow, tonight's for fun, fun, fun. The gang
have all split from the Madness dance and are jumping and bopping
around the room, Lysa has got H in her scope, she definitely going for
it tonight, she's just moving over to latch on when Superman bop's in
front of her and whispers something to H, H's face lights up, he grabs
Superman and drags him off to the kitchen, some of the gang are
looking at H and Superman disappearing into the kitchen with
quizzical looks on their faces, but there soon forgotten as Emma
finishes her song. Brian takes no prisoners, he's on the stage in a flash
looking for his next song, he smiles the smile and nods the nod as he
spots it and taps that button. Meanwhile in the kitchen, H is
absolutely fucking buzzing, He's jumping up and down and hugging
Superman, "this is gona be boss kid, they're genna love it mush",
Superman is all smiles and maybe even a sly blush as H pops his mp3
player out, "I'm gona play ye the song right an ye can memorise it",
Superman's nodding his assent as H chats on, "but it doesn't matter

right cos the words are on the screen anyway". H suddenly shuts up and simultaneously his head snaps to the kitchen door as they hear the first bars and the weird ooow aaar ooow aaaar of Bon Jovi's Living on a prayer, H looks at Superman with a huge grin "the fuckin little cunt ay, listen to wha he's singin, I've got to get in there kid, listen mush, listen to the song right, memorise it an we'll put yer on, ye gona fuckin love it kid". H gives Superman a slap on the shoulder as he heads back in. Superman pops the headphones on and pushes play on the device.

The Cave 2009.

"wooooooooooooooow we're half way thereeeeeer woooooo hooooooooo livin on a praaaaayeeeeeer", Sabretooth is up on his chair completely rat arsed, screaming his head off, he has one hand in the air and the other holding the arm of the chair for balance, but it's not giving him much aid as he's nearly come off twice. Ra's al Ghul is in his chair leaning back looking up at Sabretooth half laughing and half singing along with his chum, he sits up and reaches for the ashtray, in it is a half-smoked cone and Ra's al Ghul pops that sucker into his mouth puts lighter to cone and takes a huge drag, as he blows out a huge cloud of smoke he contemplates his new-found friend, why? Hadn't he ever really spoke to Sabretooth, had he been such an ass all these years to be so aloof and obnoxious to him. Sabretooth plops himself down in the chair and takes the joint from Ra's al Ghul, "fuck me I'm fucked, and it's only early" says Sabretooth as he takes a toke, he eases back in the chair letting his head flop back to feel the glorious room spin sensation "aaaaaaar that feels good". Ra's al Ghul is chuckling at his friend as he gets up to get more drinks, as he pops the tops from the Corona's he looks up to the screen, "O my fucking god" shouts Ra's al Ghul "he actually talked him into it". Sabretooth has still got his head back and is finding it hard to right himself, "who, did what, what?" asks Sabretooth, Ra's al Ghul turns to Sabretooth with the Corona's and hands one to him as he eventually sits up, "The Hulk my friend has succeeded in his mission, you will never guess whom has just walked on stage", a huge smile spreads across Sabretooth's mouth as Ra's al Ghul steps out of the way and the screen comes into view.

The Manor 2009 Karaoke night continued

Superman walks into the main room just as Brian is walking off stage, H's head is like a meerkat as he clocks him walking in and also spots Blade making a b-line for the stage, H is just about to shout to Blade to hang on a moment when he hears Superman's booming voice, "excuse me Mr Blade but I do believe it's my turn (he points his finger at blade) to ROCK". The gang are pissing themselves and hooting as Superman walks onto the stage, he grabs the mic and walks to the laptop, he flicks to his song as the gang all stare and wait in eager excitement, he looks up to meet H's eyes, he gives him the nod as he taps the song in. An addictive guitar riff kicks out of the speakers and most of the gang start to go crazy as they know what's coming. The rhythmic marching drum beat is next in line as Superman pops the mic into the stand and sets himself for the intro. Superman grabs the mic and stand and leans back rock god style, "I took a walk around the world to ease my troubled mind", the gang go nuts, Superman's voice is the shits, he's nails Brad Arnolds voice to a tee. Blade's asking Dave what the song is as he's the only one who's not po-going, "who's this Doyve mate", "its Kryptonite kid by Three doors down, its fuckin boss mush, listen to the lyrics he's gona sing", Blade starts a little po-going session himself as he listens to Superman. As Superman reaches the end of his verses and heads into the chorus with a "yyeeeeeeyyeeeeeeyyeeeeeee" everyone goes nuts cheering or screaming along, "If I go crazy then will you still call me Superman?

if I'm alive and well will you be there holding my hand? I'll keep you by my side with my superhuman might, Kryptonite, yeeeerrrrrr". The rooms going crazy as Lysa spots H and jumps on his back, "hey, how tee fuck did ye git him te do that" she shouts in H's ear, His loving it as he bounces her up and down, "I must av good persuasive skills girl, mustn't I" he give Lysa a cheeky grin. Superman comes off stage to a thunderous applause, he's got a massive cheeky grin all over his kipper as he spots H and b-lines over to him for a hug, "thank you H my friend that was most liberating" "I told ye you'd love it didn't I". Blade heads for the stage this time as the gang settle down skinning joints and refiling drinks. Lysa is locked into H and the conversation's good, both of them enjoying each other's company. Emma's sat next to Brodi and they're both skinning joints giving each other the fuck me eyes. The rest of the gang are bopping along with Blade, filling their glasses or skinning joints and chatting shit. The night cracks on with some unbelievable performances, all the greats are smashed on stage by the gang, Zeppelin, Beatles, Stones, Simone, Madonna, every fucker gets nailed. It's getting quite late and the songs are starting to get slow and chilled and you can tell the weed and alcohol are taking their toll, nobody is up bopping as the night nears its end. The gang are chillaxing when Blade gets up and unbeknownst to him starts an all-out Hip hop war. H is chatting to Lysa, and Dave is on the other couch with Sid and Brian when the speakers issue the sweetest baseline of the night, immediately followed by thumping silky synthesizer, H and Dave lock eyes like two bullets, their mouths wide open catching flies, Blade starts rapping to Prodigy's Waddup Gz and nails the fucker to a tee, "waddup Gz waddup Gz, it aint nottin but this murder rap, it aint nottin, aint nottin but this money stacks". Lysa is chatting something to H but he's not listening to a fucking word, his eyes and ears are on Blade pulling off his rap, H jumps up and pops and locks his way B-boy style over to Dave, "fuck me kid es fucken

nailed this cunt, but its fucken game on now mate, are ye up for it"
Dave's nodding and looking at H "fucken too rite I am mush, do ye
wana duo next kid" "too fucken right kid, you know the score, no
cunt's avin me over on me own fucken gary okey". Brian's listening to
the lads and laughing, he can't believe they're taking this so seriously,
"a way lads, are ye noo takin it a bit serioos like" asks Brian, "are you
avin a laugh Bri, don't ye know the rules of the hip hop game mush,"
H's face is stern as a mother fucker as he stares down at Brian, "the
minute someone slams a fucken rap down mate it's all out fucken
war kid, an me an Davey lad here" H thumbs over at Dave, "are the
fucken masters", H starts a little pop and lock session right in Brian's
face, he pulls of a little flashy spin and heads out on to the dance
floor to join Mel whose pulling off some sweet ass dance moves to
Blades masterpiece. Dave lights a joint as he jumps up from the
couch to join H, he turns back to Brian, " berra get ye game face on
kid cos there's gona be a fucken showdown", Dave also starts a little
pop and lock routine in Brian's face but in pure Mr Fantastic style
extends his arms and pulls off some crazy moves and then
moonwalks away with a wave, Brian and Sid are pissing themselves,
"are ye gona have a go like Sid man, do ye know any rap songs like" "
I don't know Bri, oy moght be able to knock out an owld timer mate,
whot about you mate, gonno av a go" " I dinni know man, I need a
gander at the laptoop like". As Blade come's to the end of his song
most of the gang are now back up cheering him, Dave locks eyes with
H signalling that they're next on, Brian's not even off before Dave's
up and at the laptop, as Blade walks off he passes H who gives him
the Scarface stare, "o it's on now mush" states H, Blade walks to the
gang with a confused look to his kipper, "I think yow've started a
battle like Blade man" says Brian with a smirk, he's about to say
something else when the speakers boom forth with a sweet slow
rhythmic pulse, then the beautiful but nasty guitar starts too ja ja

ja.... ja ja ja ja, Dave and H walk to the front of the stage with they're mic's in both hands Beasty boy style as the intro to the classic Beasty song Looking down the barrel of a gun pumps out. Dave screams out first as the gang go wild "aaaaaaaaaaarrrrrrrrrrrrrrrrr.......I'm rolling down the hill snowballing getting bigger", H cuts in for the second line "an explosion in the chamber, the hammer from the trigger", the boys carry on cutting in on each other with knife point accuracy, Blades giving H the not bad face as he bounces across the stage. There's no real chorus to the song but Dave and H come together for the big middle with some synchronized rapping, "looking down the barrel of a gun, son of a gun, son of a bitch getting paid getting rich". The gang are going wild as the boys come to the end of the song. Dave and H come off stage pumping fists thinking they're the shit, Blade has a huge smile on his face as he nudges past H toward the stage "not bad big man, but its game on now fucker" says Blade as he turns for the stage, but he's beaten, (to everybody's surprise) by Sid who ambles nonchalantly on to the stage. Sid only takes one step onto the stage before the room erupts "OOOOiiiiiiiiii" shouts Mel you boys av had yer chance, and there's no way yer havin a battle without me". She heads for the stage with a swagger as Sid is walking off and gives him a cheeky wink "it's all youw's me lady" says Sid as he bows offstage and on to the dancefloor. Mel hits the laptop like a woman possessed ravaging through its contents, but it only takes a second before she's tapping that button. A huge beat starts pumping from the speakers, Mel has her arms tucked in, hands by her chest boxer style and is pumping her elbows out as she shuffles to the mic. The beat is a mixture of bass drum and didgeridoo from the sublime track Mango pickle down river by M.I.A., Mel grabs the mic just in time for the opening line and pulls off the Aboriginal voices of the Wilcannia mob to a fucking tee. "when it's really hot we go to the river and swim.... when we're goin fishin we're catchin the bream......when the river's high, we jump of the bridge....and when we get home we play some didge". The gang are absolutely loving it, jumping around and doing silly aboriginal dance's, Dave bops over to H and starts a Maori haka, hilariously distorting his face, H joins in, but to be honest his is shit. Blade and Brian are pissing themselves, Brian nudges Blade, "ya think they knoo that Maori's are frum New Zealand like", Blade's pissing himself "probabli not mate, probabli not". Mel comes to the end of her song to tremendous applause, having pulled a blinder for the girls. Sid slides up on to the stage unobstructed this time and grabs the mic as he heads for the laptop, he bellows into it, "am not vewy good at rappin but I'll give it a go" he taps the laptop, and the immortal beats of a rap song, all the way from nineteen seventy-nine pumps into the room. The gang go ballistic as Sid starts to rap in his broad cockney brogue to The Sugearhill gang's Rappers delight, "a said a ip op... da ippy da ippy.... to de ip ip op an ye downt stop....de rowck it to de bang bang boogie". All the gang are loving it as Sid belts his rap out, sounding like a cockney version of the mancunian poet John Cooper Clarke, even H and Blade forget the ongoing battle to have a little dance off. Sid pulls off a blinder and is smug all over as he takes a bow. Blade's waiting like a predator for the mic as Sid comes to the end of his rap, there's no fucking way he's not going on next, and as soon as the last beat drops Blade flips onto the stage movie style and snatches the mic from Sid. He struts to the laptop knowing exactly the song he's going to pick. He flics the playlist to the letter G and punches in his bombshell. A slow melodic bluesy beat starts to flow from the speakers and a hypnotic loop of soul singer Jerry Butler kicks in. Blade grabs the mic and cuts into the song "I woke up out that coma 2001, 'bout the same time Dre dropped 2001, Three years later the album is done" and the room goes ballistic, H doesn't give a fuck he's up with Dave arms in the air screaming, he grabs Dave in a headlock "fuckin amazing mush, he's fuckin boss" Dave's pissing himself "have ye forgot about the battle then kid" shouts Dave "have I fuck mush, soon as he's finished I'm fuckin straight up" Superman's asking Brian who the song is by and Brian is asking Sid who's telling him "it's Dreams mate by The Game, fackin stormer of a song mate, and Blade's fackin nailed it mate, nailed it to a fackin tee" as Blade approaches the end of the song H is just ready to pounce when two feet land on his shoulders and an extremely nimble Lysa somersaults off H onto the stage grabbing the mic from Sid. She glances down coyly at H "sorry big fella but it's the girlies turn" Blade comes off stage and H gives him a fist bump "fuckin amazin that kid, but I'm gona smash that next mush" Blades laughing as he pats H on the back "no probs H lad, take yowr best shot" Lysa slides over to the laptop and flics to her song. She starts to rap with the first beats of the song and the gang go absolutely apeshit singing along as the chorus kicks in "my neck, my back, lick my pussy and my crack, my neck my back, lick my pussy and my crack" as Lysa sings she's looking right into the eyes of H letting him know the score. As Lysa finishes Brian tries to take the stage but H is there in the way "don't you fuckin dare wolf man, it's my stage now" H pushes Brian away and jumps to the stage, he's straight over to the laptop, flick, tap and off we go as the speakers pump out the fat assed beats of DMX's party up "Y'all gon' make me lose my mind, Up in here, up in here, Y'all gon' make me go all out, Up in here, up in here, Y'all gon' make me act a FOOL, Up in HERE, up in here, Y'all gon' make me lose my cool, Up in here, up in here" the whole room's bouncing, fucking bouncing and H thinks he's onto a winner, as he comes off he drops the mic at Brian's feet, everyone's pissing themselves as H quickly swoops the mic off the floor "only messin kid, here ye go mush, lets see what you've got" he passes the mic to Brian who slides to the laptop to make his choice. He's all fucking thumbs to be fair as he tries to pick a song and then he starts fucking talking with the mic for fucks sake "err, am not very good at rappin like, but I'll give it a goo like" his voice comes out of the mic all blurry and squealy. The bell chimes twice and then the beautiful piano riff as Eminem's The Way I am starts to pump from the speakers. Brian starts the most hideous rap you've ever herd in your life, completely and utterly destroying Eminem's song. H is well gutted, he wanted to sing this, he fucking loves it, he's fuming as he watches Brian murder the song but it gives him a moment of inspiration, he makes his way to his weed and paraphernalia first and then makes a b-line for Superman whose dancing with the girls. H starts chatting to Superman for a while and soon the duo disappear to the kitchen again. the rest of the gang are still hard at it as Brian comes off stage and the girls jump up for a trio of J Z's Hard knock life. Dave and Brian sit for a breather on the couch and to knock a few joints up and Brian's quizzing Dave again about H "I cani believe H like, he's completely changed like" "I know mate he's sound ye, but he wasn't always mush, he was a fucking nightmare in the early years to be honest, but yer he's fucking sound now" "how the fuck did that happen Davey lad, he's the fucking Hulk for fuck sake" "I know mush but yer know over the years he just stopped being angry and then ye know when yer not using your powers for years and years" "yer but man, I saw his eyes go green like Dave I fucking thought he was goni change like, thought I was a goner for sure Davey lad" Dave's laughing his head off slapping his thigh "arrrr ye killin me mush fuckin killin me, that must have been fuckin funny mush but I'll let you in on a little secret, H can't change anymore, he hasn't Hulked out for fuckin years mush, the only thing that turns green now kid is his eyes and his dick" Brian bursts out laughing "your fuckin funny Davey lad I'll give you that like" "no mush I'm serious, his eyes always go green when he's wound up they always have, his eyes are fuck all mate, and his dick, serious mate, it used to be a party trick back in the day, he'd

Hulk his dick out and we'd get loads of birds, fuckin big mad green dick, fucking boss, but then he says to me one day that he can't hulk out anymore, it's just stopped working Dave he said to me, only me dick still works mate, fucking mad" H comes back in from the kitchen and plonks himself down next to the lads "now then boys" Dave gives Brian the don't you tell him we've been chatting about him eyes and Brian nods his assent "who was that doin Run DMC while I was in there" says H "it was Brodi mush, pulled it off sound kid didn'y" answers Dave "yer he' was tops kid" "what have you been up to in there again then mush" asks Dave "fuckall kid you mind your own ay, you'll soon see" H has a cheeky little grin spreading across his kipper as he grabs the skins to roll another joint. As you may have gathered the girls had come off and Brodi had been on but it was Sid whom was back up at the moment, he was about half way through his rendition of Ice-Ice Baby and Blade and the girls were all up dancing. As H skins his joint up he watches Blade whom looks as though he's just having a bop, but H is on to the fucker, H can see him stalking the stage ready to pounce the second Sid finishes. H watches Blade like a hawk, but himself pretending to be concentrating on building his joint, and just as Sid goes to deliver his last line H pounds Hulk style over the heads of everyone, lighting his newly built joint mid flight and landing on the stage just as Sid drops his last "too cold" and snatches the mic "touché H, nice move, now let's see what yow've got" shouts Blade from the floor. H slides over to the laptop again knowing the exact song he wants, he taps in his selection. The gang look quite confused as a Coldplay guitar riff starts up but are soon clicking on as H blasts out with the beginning of Rick Ross's Hustlin, H starts the rap deep voiced sounding sweet "who the fuck you think you fucking with? I'm the fucking boss" the guys are going crazy, even Blade loving it rapping along, but H pulls a blinder after the first chorus when he switches rick's song to the Plan B version from the

Mixtape album, flipping to Bens voice with pure perfection "Yeah I'm always hustlin' blud, I'm hustlin' even when, I'm just sitting in the flat, sipping on a Jack, chilling with my girlfriend" the gang are going wild for the Plan B rap and the whole crew's up now bopping away. H is nearing the end and Blade's deffo up next standing ready to pounce, but just as H finishes and Blade starts too take the stage all three girls put hands to blade "where do ya think your going big fella, it's us girls now" Blades laughing and shaking his head as he admits defeat again and lets the girls to the stage, Mel slides to the laptop, flicks to the choice and the immortal eighties beatbox sound of Salt and Peppers push it pulses out of the speakers. The girls are on form as all three take up a mic each as blast out "Ooh, baby, baby

Baby, baby, Ooh, baby, baby, Baby, baby, get up on this" Blade has his arm around H shouting down his ear "yow did the fuckin business with that last one H, but I'm gona crush yow when I eventually get up there" as Blade is chatting to H he doesn't realise that the girls are nearing the end of their song and to blades utter annoyance misses his chance again as Dave jumps up "the Davey train is in the building fuckers" he shouts as he grabs the mic. He glides to the laptop tapping his selection and once again the gang go nuts as the collaboration from T.I. and Eminem starts to blast out from the speakers. Dave pulls the song off to a tee switching from T.I. to Eminem and back again, but it's when he gets to the mega fast rapping of Eminem that the gang go apeshit for Dave "Life is too short and I got no time to sit around just wasting it, So I pace this shit a little bit quicker, that clock, I'm racing in doubling time it, But I still spit triple the amount of insults in a tenth of the time" Dave pulls the rap off to thunderous shouts from the mob as he bows his way of stage, Blade is not getting blown off this time and jumps up, he's just about to take the mic when a red flash swoops around the room and the mic disappears only to reappear next to Blade in Superman's hand "I do believe this stage belongs to me bitch" shouts Superman at Blade, the gang are pissing themselves as they watch Blade admit defeat once more and climb from the stage as Superman picks his song out "I'm going to need the assistance of one of you beautiful young ladies please" shouts Superman, Lysa's loving it as she screams her way to the stage to help the big man out. A beautiful hypnotic guitar riff pumps from the speakers with a sweaty fat base as Eminem's Superman starts from the speakers, Lysa starts in with the oooo's and aaaaar's just as Superman smashes in with his lyrics, he's feeling absolutely fabulous now as all mental health problems disappear with the drugs, music and friends, the gang absolutely apeshit as they know exactly what's coming, Superman pulls Eminem off to a tee and as he hits the bridge the whole room erupts with him "but I do know one thing though, bitch's they come they go, Saturday through Sunday, Monday, Monday through Sunday yo, maybe I'll love you one day, maybe we'll someday grow, till then just sit your drunk ass on that fuckin' runway ho 'cause I can't be your Superman, can't be your superman, can't be your superman, can't be your superman" Dave's got H in a headlock rubbing his head "fuckin stroke of genius that kid fuckin boss" he's telling H "you know the score kid when it comes to the music H is yer man" as Superman comes to the end of his hit Blade's taking no prisoners this time as he takes to the stage and grabs the mic "yow can sit for this number if yow want, knock a few joints up refill yowr glasses" the beautiful guitar riff from Stings Shape of my heart starts up and the whole room applauds Blades choice as Blade cuts in with Nas's lyrics. Most of the guys do sit as Brian's choice is a smooth ass hip hop ride of emotion one of the greatest hip hop songs ever. H sits down to enjoy and has a quick go of a bong to enjoy the song. Lysa slides over to H and just sits with him enjoying the song, in fact all the group end up completely silent watching Blade from the couch do his stuff like a pro "I never sleep, cause sleep is the cousin of death, I aint the type of brother made for you to start testing, I never sleep, cause sleep is the cousin of death" as Blade finishes the gang erupt and are all gutted it's over, H jumps up and grabs Blade "fuckin amazin that kid fuckin amazin, you wun this battle by a fuckin mile with that shit kid, fuckin boss" Blade gets all embarrassed now as he sits down for a well earned joint. As all the guys attention was on Blade coming off stage they hadn't noticed that Brian had once again hit the laptop and only realised as the fat piano hook from Jay-Z and Linkin Park's Numb pounds from the speakers, the gang are a little apprehensive from Brian's earlier attempt but the drugs and the music have mellowed Brian out completely and just like Superman the dude is on fire, plus it's absolutely the perfect song to accompany Blade's masterpiece.

The Cave 2009.

"I've become so numb, I can't feel you there, become so tired, so much more aware, by becoming this all I want to do, Is be more like me and be less like you" Ra's al Ghul and Sabretooth are swaying in the cave, arms around each other, loved up, pissed, stoned and fucking loving the karaoke night, their voices raw from the constant howling "o my friend this has been the best night ever, I can't remember the last time I was having this much fun" shouts Ra's "the night is but young Ra's, imagine the delights we still have to come" a huge smile spreads across Ra's face as he grabs his friend in another hug-lock "too fucking right big fella" we slide out of the room as the two new friends howl with laughter and enjoyment, out of the doors and along a huge corridor where blinking overhead lights make the rock walls look super spooky, the cave tunnel we slide along is so immense it's a long time before we reach the door of Spiderman and glide through. Spiderman sits at his desk now finished with his nights main work but still tinkering. He has his screens tuned to the manor and karaoke night, but unlike our two friends in the monitor room, Spiderman is not enjoying himself "fucking dirty fucking shitty fucking marvellous cunts, the day cannot come sooner, that fucking useless green twat can't even change anymore, ha, ha, wait until I tell the boss that little treat, thinks he's a rocker and a rapper, fucking retard, don't know why the boss was ever scared of the prick, I always told him we could take him anyway, green or not fucking green" he sits hateful allowing his mental health to evolve, his depressions deepen, fuck it and fuck them all he's thinking as he takes a huge toke on a joint, he gets up and goes to his CD rack tracing his finger down the ribs until one speaks to him, he pulls the CD from the rack and pops it into his super sound system and presses play "now this is fucking music fuckers" the amazingly beautiful first notes of the Eddie Vedder album Into the Wild break into the silence like light into dark, and it spreads instantly into the depressed and morbid ears of Spiderman, and with the mix of potent cannabis Spiderman beds down for a beautiful night of glorious depression.

The Manor 2009 Karaoke night continued.

There's been many more hip-hop karaoke whilst we've been on our little detour and the gang are juiced up to fuck to be fair. The nights starting to clock on and the music has taken a slower and groovier slide to suit the mood of the gang. Emma's up doing the Duffy number Breath Away (she keeps giving Brodi the eye, and he's fucking loving it) most of the gang are sitting now, skinning up mixing drinks and catching up. Lysa's sitting with H catching up and flirting, but to the annoyance of both of them, Brian's there with them interrupting and basically being a cunt. Sid, Dave, Blade and Mel are chatting with Superman about who sent the invites. Dave keeps flirting with Mel and can't figure out if she's up for it or not, but he's defo going to try his luck later. Sid keeps reverting back into a slight depression about all those poor girls he violated, he's opened up to a few of the gang now and they're all basically saying the same thing, to just chill out, destroy all the shit, there's a little beast in all of us at times, so just make it up to them later the best way you can, Sid's thinking that it's going to be a fucking lot of making up, but he's up for it and the thought brings him back up, giving him something to focus on. Emma comes of stage and Blade jumps up, he hits his song on the laptop and the beautiful guitar from Al Green's how can you mend a broken heart kicks in, the next sound to invade our ears are the soulful strings and Blades amazing voice. Lysa snuggles into H and Brian suddenly gets the point and moves over to the boys. Emma's planted herself next to Brodi, she's asking him what they're all talking about, and Brodi's letting Emma know. Emma's laughing "who gives a fack guys, just enjoy it for fack sake, we're all together, what the fack can happen to us" a few of the guys are nodding in agreement, Dave's thinking, I didn't really give a fuck, I'm livin it up in this fucker. Superman on the other hand just can't shake the dreaded feeling, something is amiss, he just can't put his finger on it. Blade comes off and Mel jumps up to do a Prince number, Joy in Repetition, she pulls the song off in her own sassy style, some of the guys jump up for sexy time dancing, it's fucking hilarious. Lysa takes the opportunity to front H "hey big fella do ye fancy slippin away" H's eyes nearly pop the fuck out, he's nodding like a dog "too fuckin right I do girl" Lysa grabs H's hand and the sneak away (well they think they do but to be fair every-cunt watches them go) Dave's buzzing for his mucka as he watches H scuttle off with Lysa, fuckin lucky fucker he's thinking, he's also thinking that he's going to have a crack at Mel. Most of the others are just smirking to themselves, there'll be plenty more of that going on their thinking, we haven't seen each other for years, and any barriers we had have been well and truly fucking blown to smithereens. Mel comes off stage and Brian dives up and does a

Gomez number, We Haven't Turned Around, and does it well, Dave's proper buzzing "this is one of me favourite songs ever this girl" Mel fresh off stage is immediately set on by Dave trying his luck. Lysa's whispering to Brodi "shall we err, scuttle off soon?" Brodi's fucking buzzing "yer girl, I'll go to the kitchen for something and scoot out the side, whose room we meetin in?" "knock a few joints up and I'll meet you in your room" whispers Lysa with a wink. Sid's chatting to Superman about the mansion again, he seems to be the only one with Superman to be concerned "I don't like it me-self big man, the whole thing don't make sense" they decide it has to be one of their old adversary's but they can't decide or agree one which one. Brodi gets up and goes into the kitchen, nobody really notices and as Brian comes off stage Lysa jumps up "this is me last one guys then I'm off to bed" she punches her selection in and the speakers preach, O they preach baby, a beautiful funky guitar pounds out, it's Moby's The Right Thing and Lysa's voice is amazing. Mel immediately jumps up, even though it's a slow song and she's rocking away. Blade's plops himself next to Dave and has started rolling a massive cone. Dave, taking his eyes off Mel's ass for a second notices blade's nearly built cone "fuckoff Bri, that's fucking boss mush, a proper fucking cone mate, you'll have to teach me that one mush" Blade's made up "yer no probs Duve, I'll knock another up now and yow can watch" Blade gives the cone to Dave to light as he starts to build another and illustrate at the same time, Dave lights the big ass cone and sucks a huge deep lung full of skunk, as he blows the smoke out he pulls off the old stoned again face for Blade (you know the poster and t-shirt from the eighties where the cartoon fella melts) and Blade's in stitches "that's fucking top notch that is Duve, fuckin brill" Lysa comes off stage and shuts her goodnights to everyone that's left "I'm gona go with you love" says Mel as she too shouts her goodnights. Dave's proper pissed off but shouts his goodnights with a smile "thought I was in their lads, thought I was in" he's shaking his head and having a little laugh with himself. Superman to the surprise of everyone walks up to the stage without saying a thing and grabs the mic. Elvis's Are you Lonesome Tonight struts through the speakers, Superman's silky voice mimics the king beautify. Sid joins Dave and Blade for a who can do the best joint compo and Brian's in like Flynn also. It's a weird scene, Dave chonging on a massive cone as he builds another, Sid chugging on a joint as he tries to build a tulip joint, Blade chonging on his new cone, Brian lighting an old roach left in the ashtray and Superman in the background singing a fucking Elvis song.

The Cave 2009

The lads are absolutely fucked, lying spread eagled on the Magneto comfy chairs chugging on their last joints, lukewarm drink in hand hanging over the side, "best night ever bra, best night ever" mumbles Sabretooth as he passes out, his drink hitting the floor and rolling into numerous other bottles and cans on the floor. Ra's al Ghul, eyes rolling, head swaying backward, is laughing looking at Sabretooth, he takes a huge pull on a tiny joint and blows out the smoke in a huge eddy. He turns again to laugh at Sabretooth but instead throws up, it's not to bad only a little hits Sabretooth on his lolling arm. Ra's immediately passes out across his comfy chair, and to be fair not a second to soon because Magneto swans in, back from his little trip. He's in a good mood luckily, but still hit the fucking roof when he spots his so called brothers "fucking useless fucking bastards" he's about to wake them, maybe crush them a little in their comfy chairs, but tonight he's just not feeling it "I'll see you pair of fucking useless fuckers in the morning" he storms off down the rock corridor, he's wondering if he should go see his friend Spiderman but the hour is late "fuck it they can all wait for Manana, it's bed time" as he walks to his room he thinks he can hear something coming from the back entrance, but that door has never been used, and from the outside you can't even see it. Magneto heads along the corridor hearing the sound getting louder, as he goes around a corner he lets out a girly scream throwing his hands up, but only for a second, she was just standing there, like a fucking zombie, like that fucking girl in the movie The Ring he comes to his senses and realises she been battered absolutely beat to a pulp "O MY FUCKING GOD, Enchantress what has happened? where have you been? Who did this to you? The Enchantress's eyes flutter open for a moment "Magneto" is all she can muster before she passes out.

The Manor 2009 karaoke night continued.

Dave's up onstage singing the Scott Matthews song elusive, the lads are all sitting in a line smoking "right lads" shouts Sid "I'm off to bed, I'm facked" and with that he gives a shaky wave and wobbles off to bed. Brian pours the lads new drinks and they all clink, Dave comes down and joins them "anyone else having a go" all the lads are pretty much fucked now and are shaking their heads "nar fuck it, were fucked" Dave's laughing, "fuck it then I'm smoking this and hitting the sack, wha are you lot up to then" "I never sleep really Dave" says Superman "me neither big man" says Blade as he elbows Superman "do yow fancy watchin some movies then Sup, or maybe a game of pool" Superman's well up for it and Brian asks if he can join them "yow don't have to ask mate" says blade, the lads finish the joints and drinks they have, Dave exits stage left for bed and the boys head for the cinema. The boys can't believe that Superman has never seen what his little chat with Stan Lee had spawned, and they've told him he's getting a crash course "yow've got some catching up to do Sup" says Blade as he slaps Superman on the back. The lads get themselves proper comfy in the cinema with drinks popcorn and lots of weed.

Dave flops down onto is duvet and lets out a huge sigh, he's still got half a joint in his mouth, he pulls out his lighter and lights it taking a huge drag. As he's lying there he starts to think about Mel and how fit she looked tonight, his dick starts to swell as he's thinking of that ass and as usual his penis starts to take control of his mind. His hand slides down and he gives his cock a squeeze, she was loving the attention tonight he's thinking, fucking loving it. He's hard as a rock now thinking of all the flirting they'd been doing earlier, I recon she'll be well up for a little pokey-pokey. Dave lets go of his dick, it slides over the edge of the bed and drops, thub, it hits the floor and heads for the door. When Dave's bell-end reaches the door, it flattens out and slithers under popping out the other side, it looks up with it's one eye and caries on down the hall like a scene from Jaws heading for Mel's room. Dur dum, dur dum, d, d, d, d, d, d, dur, dum, he reaches Mel's room and flattens out again.

Mel's in her room lying on her bed, she's sipping on a Jack and Coke and occasionally taking a toke from a cone that Blade had made for her. Her headphones are on and she's listening to Nina Simone, as she takes her joint from the ashtray she spies something coming under the door and nearly crying with laughter as she watches Dave's bell-end pop up, it slithers in feeling its way around and Mel gets a cheeky little look in her eye. She runs to the dresser and grabs her hair tongs, runs back and plugs them in, she dives back in bed just in time as Dave's dick comes over the top of the bottom of the bed, his one eye seeming to look around, Mel's even wondering if he can see with that thing but then no, he's sniffing around like a dog. Mel decides to have just a little more fun than she should, she loves Dave, he's a cheeky gorgeous little ball o fun and she had a ball with him tonight, but she's not up for a fuck though just a bit of fun, she watching Dave's dick and is getting quite excited, she takes off her sloggy's, takes a huge toke of her joint and lies down getting herself ready. Dave's dick slithers slowly up the bed, he touches her leg and she nearly screams laughing but holds it in, she relaxes, Dave's bell end reaches Mel's amazing pussy, shaven as usual except for a sweet-ass little Mohican, he touches her lips and jerks back like a child taking a sweet that knows it shouldn't. Mel's watching him giggling away, but as Dave moves in she takes a last toke on her joint and lies her head back. Dave's bell-end moves in, he rubs up against the crevice between her thigh and pussy lip, moving up and over her fat mound. Mel's loving it, it's like a velvet massage. Dave moves down over Mel's pussy and gently rubs across her man in the boat, it sends a shiver of electric-extasy and excitement through Mel's whole body and as Dave's bell-end arrives at Mel's lips there's little a pearl drop of love juice waiting. He slides over her lips, parting them gently and Mel quivers again. She lets Dave play around for a minute but then that cheeky smile returns when she senses he's about to go all in, she waits for a second, Dave's bell's rubbing in a circle around her lips, he stops right in the centre and gives a slight push, his bell-end slides in easily but only half way, he pulls back out and repeats a couple of times. Mel's loving it, but enough is enough she can't lead the poor fella on too much. so just as Dave for the first time pushes his dick up into that glorious wet pussy.

Dave's bell-end reaches Mel's door and back in his room lying on his bed he's thinking yer this is the door it was deffo three doors down, he slides under and into the room slowly going from left to right looking around blindly. He feels the leg of the bed and glides up, coming over the top and onto the mattress, he slithers up slowly, cautiously until suddenly he hits something, a pussy, O my good god, a pussy, it was it was, he cautiously goes back in feeling the crevice of her thigh. As Dave plays around for a while he grows and grows in confidence, she's fucking loving this, fucking loving it, her juices are flowing like fuck. He has a few prods to test the water and then it's hey ho here we go. Dave pushes into Mel's pussy and It's the sweetest most velvety most

WWWHHHHAAAAAAARRRRRRRRRRRRRR...AAAAAARRRRRRRR

Mel carefully places the tongs around Dave's dick as it slides into her pussy, and just when he hits the spot she clamps down on that fat dick, holding on for dear life. Dave has never experienced anything like this in his life, from sheer extasy to excruciating pain. The moment Mel did whatever she's doing Dave has been bucking like a fucking wild bronco, but he knows he's still inside Mel's pussy he can feel it through the pain, that beautiful silky wet pussy, but the pain, the fucking pain. Dave's guttural scream has changed slightly now with a mixed tone of extasy, so Mel doesn't feet as bad now as she rides that dick like a fucking Ducati, gripping the tongs even harder as she climaxes hard, she's screaming louder than Dave now and three doors down he actually has a smile. She lets the last of her shudders pass and realises she's still holding the tongs tight as fuck, o fuck it she thinks, I'll have to say thanks. Dave's at that point, his load is half way up the tube but not all the way, it must be the pain he's thinking, he knows Mel has just cum her load, he felt it and heard it, he feels the tongs removed and Mel sliding off and his load slips a little closer. The next thing he feels sends him into overdrive, it's Mel's icy cold lips as she uses her powers then mouth enclose around his bell-end and down around the burn, cooling it instantly. Dave lasts about two seconds more and Mel feels it, she pulls off just in time to see Dave's load flying out, and fuck me is it a load, Mel cracks on until it's all out for the poor fucker, poor cunt mustn't have had his hole in years thinks Mel as she heads for the en-suite for the cleaning products. Dave lies in bed slithering his poor fucked up dick back home. He has to hold it up so the burn doesn't touch the floor, it looks like a strange walking stick, it eventually arrives and Dave relaxes, but shaking like a fucker "what the fuck just happened" he picks up his roach from the bed, dropped a long time ago and lights it, there's only a few tokes but fuck me are they good.

None of the lad's downstairs heard the commotion upstairs as the movie was on too loud, but Brodi and Emma heard it alright but they just thought it was one or two of the gang having fun like them just a little louder. H on the other hand knew his muckers war cry and tensed up the moment it went air-bourn, but Lysa held on like a woman possessed "leave him it's cool" she whispers as she flips him over and gets on-top making sure there's no escape. As Dave's crys turn slightly from pain to joy she whispers again just to reassure "see he's loving it now, whatever it is there up to" H relents and leaves his buddy to the fate of the universe. Sid's lying in his room smoking a joint and watching a bit of telly when he hears Dave's cry's he's immediately relived because from the sound of it he's now not the only beast in the house, because the only thing that would make you scream like that is a dick injury, Sid's heard that cry before, he lies back and gets comfortable, relief flooding in, his joint tasting sweeter his brandy tasting sharper, good times he's thinking, good times.

The Cave 2009.

Magneto sits by the bed of the Enchantress holding her hand. He's looking at her beat up face, he'd carried her here to his makeshift surgery and tried the best that he could to mend her, eventually admitting defeat. He'd gone to the local hospital and kidnaped (in front of everyone, not caring one iota) one of the best surgeons there. Flying in on his disc and back out again surgeon in toe he was back in the cave in no time. The surgeon, obviously fucking frazzled, first of all getting kidnaped by a lunatic on a flying disc, second actually flying with said lunatic at fuck-knows miles per hour. Then placed in front of what can only be described as, well? A Superwoman of some kind. He's then told to fix this superbeing and to be fair she is pretty fucked up. He tells Magneto that they will have to undress her and is subsequently called all the dirty, nasty fucking perv… "NO, Mr whoever you are, we have to check her extensively, god Knows what she looks like if her face is anything to go by" Magneto relents and the surgeon goes to work exposing the full spectrum of The Enchantress's injuries and abrasions. The surgeon, although never working with something or some body like this before is amazing, he glides around her body calling to Magneto, telling him what should and needs be done here and there. "she's unbelievable, I've never seen anything like it before, she's healing herself at an expeditious rate, but look here" the surgeon points to an arm that is severely bent out of shape "if we don't fix these quickly she'll heal badly, twisted and bent, here now, make a metal cast for this" the surgeon bends on the twisted arm and snaps it back into place as Magneto moulds super-soft metal casts to fit perfectly. As the surgeon glides around the Enchantress fixing and pointing for casts and splints. He watches Magneto, transfixed as he moulds with the metal in the room, seeming to sense the metal, he reaches and with the slightest movement of his fingers brings the metal to himself from around the room, the metal, with a consistency that looks allot like gasses floating through the air to wisp down and transform into the cast of Magnetos choice. When the two men are finished fixing her broken bones they clean and wrap Enchantress and place her in a super-comfy metal form bed that caresses her like a womb. Magneto stands at the edge of the bed, he call's a chair over from the other side of the room, the chair gliding past the surgeon that Magneto has already forgotten about straight into the hands of the metal god. Magneto sits into the chair never taking his eyes from the woman in front of him. The surgeon purses his lips and takes a look around the room, there's a door to the left just behind him, he tiptoes backward through and out of the door into a strange cave like hallway, he looks around as he walks stumbling slightly in the strange cave as only a few scattered lights overhead flicker making him feel like he's in an old horror movie. The surgeon feels like he's been walking forever, he's already passed two smaller looking corridors' but decided to carry on in this main vain, suddenly a huge cavern opens out before him and before he reaches the opening he dashes to the cave wall trying to conceal himself. He peers into the huge room glimpsing a wall of tv monitors that show a mansion and all the rooms in it, the only thing moving on the screens is a screen itself showing some superhero movie of some kind. His eyes glide down to a strange looking console unit and then two very large and very strange looking men comatose in chairs, the chairs surrounded by a sea of bottles and but ends. The surgeon slowly and silently backs out from the room not knowing what to do, thinking that he'll have to take one of the earlier tunnels. He reaches the first shaft and cautiously enters sliding his hand along the wall for purchase and comfort, the feel of the wall making him safe for some unknown reason. He suddenly reaches a door and does a stupid little dance on his feet out of excitement and fear not knowing what to do, there must be a way out of hear he's thinking as he turns the handle. The surgeon enters another dark room and closes the door letting his eyes adjust to the dark, he takes a few trepid steps into the room as it starts to come into focus, a bedroom, he's in a bedroom, the surgeon looks around taking in his surroundings, a huge room that looks like it belongs to a teenager with all the rock god posters and CD racks and DVD's. WHAAAAAAAAAAAAAAAAAA goes the surgeon as the upside-down face of Spiderman appears directly in front "ssssorry did I ssscare you" says the muffled voice as the surgeon faints to the floor. Spiderman drops from his vine to the floor and straightens up over the strange man "and who pray tell are you my friend"

The Manor 2009 chill out day

Arrrr yes, back in the manor, it's early doors and we're floating through the huge seventeenth century mammoth like a movie scene. We start in the cinema where the guys have been catching Superman up on all the comic book antics of the past, they gave him a quick intro on the early movies like Superman, Batman, Spiderman (Superman was horrified to find out that Spiderman had been depicted as a superhero "but he was despicable, the worst of them all I would say" he'd said to the others) but moved on to the new movies such as X Men, Hulk, Iron Man and The Fantastic four. Superman is in heaven, transfixed, laying back popcorn all over himself, he hasn't taken his eyes of the screen, the other two on either side of him have been asleep for ages. We back out and turn through to the hall and pass Brodi on the way as he goes to the cinema to see what the boys are up to, but we glide on through to the kitchen to see H knocking up all kinds of good stuff for breakfast, Sid sits at the table chatting away to H "some fackin night that was ay H, oy haven't laughed that much in ages, or sang for that matter" "I know mush, it's madness how we've only all just met up" H starts placing some of the breaky on the table, he turns and we follow him into the communal room "come on girls, breakys ready" Lysa and Emma are spread across the couches giggling and whispering "ok big fella we're coming now" H turns back into the kitchen as we leave him, we float across the communal room and head for the stairs and up. We only have to get to the top because Dave and Mel have come out of their rooms together meeting at the top of the stairs, Dave's a little bit coy at first daring his eyes to meet hers "err sorry about that last night girl, but err, can I just tell ye that err, look, that was the weirdest, hornyest most unbelievable thing that's ever happened to me" Mel's laughing her head off "don't you worry about it babe I had to give you a little spanking for being cheeky but it all worked out cool in the end big fella" she gives his todge a little squeeze as she seductively slips by and down the stairs "you comin for breaky big man" she gives him a little wink and Dave's after her like a flash. We follow the big man down and into the communal room where the girls are just getting up and heading for the kitchen "morning girls" says Mel as she joins her female companions, the three all giggly as the enter the kitchen and take seats followed closely by Dave "I'm just goin to see if the boys want any breaky" says H as he leaves through the other door. Sid's looking around the room at the faces trying to decide whom was making all the commotion last night, but to be fair it could have been any of the fuckers. Everyone tucks into H's full English, fuckin doorstops, bacon, hash browns, beans, sauntered mushrooms, sausage, black pud, tomato, and three types of egg, pancakes, crumpets, bagels the fucking lot, it's like a fucking zoo to be honest. H has crept into the cinema to see if he can frighten anyone but is immediately knocked off his tracks, on the giant screen is H is looking at himself as Superman watches Ang Lee's masterpiece Hulk. H forgets all about giving them the frighteners and slots himself down next to Brodi "now then mush breaky's ready if anyone wants some" Brodi whispers back "these two are still asleep" he thumbs at Blade and Brian "and there's no fucking way you're getting Super-bollocks out of here, the fucker nearly fucking killed me before for asking how's it going" H is pissing himself as he dares press pause on the DVD player. He wakes the lads and asks if they want food and they're out the door like hot shit on a skateboard. "nice one H lad I'll leave you with the big man, I'm fucking starving" whispers Brodi as he slides out of his seat. H slides over to Superman and whispers "there's breakfast in the kitchen if your hungry big man, or do you want me to bring some in for ye" "no thank you H" whispers Superman "I'm fine, I'm just going to watch the end of this epic movie about you, it's nearly finished I think" H looks up to the screen "fuck me mush if ye like this one mush wait till you see the next one, it's fuckin well better" "thank you H I will put it in my list, I have lots to watch still, I haven't even watched the Blade trilogy yet" he turns to H for the first time ripping his eyes from the screen "but don't tell him, he fell asleep so…" "no need to be like that big man the Hulk's fuckin well better than Blade" H gives Superman a few rib ticklers with his elbow until he sees the caped crusader sprout a tiny grin "I'll leave you to it then Sup an I'll make sure there's some left for ye" "thank you H, I wont be long" H slides out of his seat and tiptoes out of the cinema leaving Superman to his movies, he heads for the kitchen where the whole gang are now congregated. Dave looks up as H enters the kitchen "now then mush" shouts Dave, H takes a seat wearing a huge grin "mornin big man, sleep well?" he gives Dave a sly look that says you can tell me later about your night.

The Cave 2009.

Spider man creeps along the tunnel, he reaches the door to the makeshift infirmary and hesitates not wanting to believe what the human had told him. He'd webbed him to the wall and brought him round out of his mini coma, the human had told him everything about what had happened, the man kidnaping him and whisking him off on a metal disc, about the woman, the healing. As Spiderman roared with anger the human had urinated, and for that he was knocked back to the land of nod. Spiderman drops from the ceiling, flips and lands in full Spiderman pose, he enters the room full on stealth mode but the master, the man, Magneto hadn't moved an inch, still holding the hand of the Enchantress. Spiderman edges closer until he's at the bed, Magneto turns for the first time and acknowledges his friend, but he doesn't make a sound just turns back to his Enchantress. They sit there for what could be hours before finally Magneto talks "she's been gone for so long, I thought I'd never see her again" "she's back now boss and all mended by the looks of it, you can relax" "relax yes... that is until she wakes my friend" Magneto turns eyes burning and grabs Spiderman "and I fucking burn whoever did this"

A good way down the hall Ra's al Ghul stirs from his slumber groggily focusing on the carnage around the room, he gets up and shakes Sabretooth until he comes round "come my friend shake your slumber off we must clean this mess" the two men shake their hangovers away and hurriedly clean the room "what shall we do now boss?" asks Sabretooth "I am not your boss friend remember that" Ra's puts his hand on his friends shoulder "we shall go to our rooms until called upon, we should act as normal" Ra throws his hands up with a look of sudden enlightenment on his face "we haven't done anything anyway" he slaps sabretooth on the back as they depart down one of the tunnels for their lodgings.

The Manor 2009

When the credits start to roll on the humongous screen in the cine room Superman stands up and gives himself a fucking good stretch "wwwhhhhaaaaarrrrrrrrr... that feels good" he strides out of the cinema and spies the girls going into the communal room "good morning ladies, I hope you all slept well, I have been catching up on the superhero movies" "mornin Sup" shout the girls in unison" "what ye been watchin then" shouts Mel "arr, I haven't seen you girls yet but I'm about to watch the X Men trilogy and Wolverine Origins, apparently it's only just came out, I can't wait to see you girls in action" the girls are pissing themselves "go on Sup lad your gona love them" the girls retire to the couches with massive fresh brewed coffee and start rolling joints and chatting. Superman enters the kitchen and is greeted with the most delightful smells "o my goodness H you really have outdone yourself this looks delightful" "arrrr ye nice one Sup, dig in lad, this is all yours we've all had enough mush" Superman sits down and starts to stack a plate, H pours Superman a fresh jug of coffee as the lads carry on chatting "I enjoyed your film immensely H and Brian I am abut to watch the X Men so I will soon see you in action" "when you gona watch Supaman returns like" asks Brian "ha, ha yes Brian I am saving it for later" the lads are all laughing and Dave nudges his mucka "so err, how did it go then" Dave's nodding his head in the direction of the communal room and H is pissing himself "fuckinell kid could you be a little more subtle" all the lads are laughing "come on H" they're all shouting "all right all right fuckinell, well it was boss like you know good night an that, I nearly fucked it up like" Dave's pissing it "I knew you'd fuck it up, fuckin Mystique" H is laughing looking at Dave "you know what appened cos you'd have done the same ye cunt" all the lads are looking at each other confused "come on then H lad spit it out" "ok, ok, I couldn't make me mind up lads and it nearly backfired" "fuckinell are yow goin on about H" asks Blade "ye know lads, we go upstairs and we're getting a bit frisky an that and she says to me, I can change into anyone you want you know, who would you like me to be big boy, well, you know me kid, I couldn't choose, I went through fuckin loads of birds, supermodels, actresses, singers, fuckin English birds fuckin yanks, she got a right cob on in the end, I had to use the old faithful, you know I asked her to use her own form, I told her she was more beautiful than all of them and it seemed to work" the lads are all laughing "I never really thought of that H, fuckinell any woman in the world, fuck me I wouldny be able to choose either H lad" says Brian. H points his finger at Dave "anyway bollocks" he says to Dave "what was all the fuckin racket from your end then, an don't act all innocent tellin me you stubbed yer fuckin toe or something" all the lad's heads swivel in Dave's direction, eyes wide "arrrr, that was you then Dave" states Sid with a sly grin. Dave's all coy as he looks to H and then around the lads "sorry boys it's a little bit embarrassing at the minute" he looks to H "I'll tell you later kid" and a little wink let H know that there's going to be a tale and a half later. Most of the lads haven't got a clue what they're talking about anyhow, it's only Sid who's still sitting with a grin having not only heard Dave's wails but Mel's also, someone was being a naught boy alright he's thinking and once again it cheers him right up and he's glad of the fact that he's not the only beast in the house "what about you then Brodi lad any tales to brighten our mornin" asks Dave trying to divert the attention elsewhere "sorry lads but there's no kissing and telling from me, you'll just have to use your imagination" Superman's looking around the room as he fills his belly, he thinks he knows what the lads are gabbing about but he's not a hundred percent, he's imagining the lads have been having fun with the girls and why not they are grown adults and to be fair he's not really arsed anyhow he's just dying to get back to the cinema "err excuse me fellows but err when I've finished eating I was going to go back to the cinema but I didn't want to be ignorant and..." "ay don't you fuckin dare mush" shouts H "you do whatever you want kid we've got all the time in the world here Sup, no-one thinks like that, we all love a good movie kid and you've got some catching up to do mush so you just crack on kid, you do whatever you want" "thank you men that's most comforting, thank you I am learning much from the movies, but I was also wondering if any of you have any of those strange cigarettes we were smoking last night, I do believe it would complement the movies somewhat" the gang are properly laughing now all looking around at each other "too fuckin right they do Sup" shouts Sid and the next thing you know there's now a competition to build Superman the perfect joint for his movies, Blade starts to knock a cone up Dave starts another tulip "err boys I only wanted one you know" "Sup lad you'll be in there all fuckin day big man your goni need a shitload son" says Brian "well, you all seem to know what your talking about, I'll let you guys sort it all out" "fuckin too right you will mush, I might even join you for the first movie lad" says H "yer to be fair lads what are we goin to do with the day, chill out, watch movies with Sup?" asks Dave "yer Dave lad that sounds tops, a nice chill out day on the couches and that maybe get the guitars out and that" "fuckin boss Blade lad you've hit the fuckin nail on the edd mush, a nice chillout day fuckin guitars an that, I'm fuckin lovin that mush that's our day well sorted out.

The Cave 2009.

Spiderman's initial anger and disappointment has dissipated, when he first heard from the human and came into the room he was full of it, but after seeing Enchantress (and he did love Enchantress, they were very good friends, he just didn't like being number three) lying beaten nearly dead on that table, and the boss, the main man, the gaffer, the strongest man Spiderman has ever known reduced to this, all he felt now was the anger and malice, the same anger and malice that was emanating from the boss and all he was waiti... "ater, cough, cough, lease water" the two men had been sitting there so long both had been in sleepy trances, both had missed her eyes flutter, her lips part, but neither missed those first sputtered words. Spiderman like a flash webs a bottle of water from across the room and hands it to the boss before she'd even finished said sputter. Magneto holds her head as he gently lets the water find its course on her mouth, as always a slight trickle runs from her lip, it rolls down her chin and onto her top, she feels it and gives Magneto the dreaded stare, Spiderman sees Magneto's little err and the evil glare she gives him for it, he watches the grin on Magnetos face spread "o she's back, yes she's back" whispers Magneto as he dabs her chin. There's a weird warm excitement building in Spiderman, he can feel the plans of the past few years culminating and avalanching down into one sublime moment of death and chaos at the sight of the Enchantress "who did this to you my love, who would do such a thing" the Enchantress's eyes flutter open closed open closed, rolling whites blue whites blue, eventually steadying fixed. The Enchantress tries to speak groggily but Magneto grabs her hand "don't vex yourself my dear all will come in good time" he whispers it cautiously but Spiderman can tell the Enchantresses powers are returning, he can feel it, actually! he can see it. The Enchantress with a sudden burst of remembrance and energy grabs Magneto, "the army, the government, I went searching... herd they had others held captive... friends from our past..." her eyes widen as she pulls Magneto closer, harder, "they knew... tortured me... they know." Her eyes flutter closed as her grip weakens and her head falls back to the pillow. For a few seconds Spiderman looks like a pidgin as his head flicks form Magneto to Enchantress sending those tiny electrical signals of total angered excitement, they curse from his brain down into every nerve ending as his eyes rest on Magneto. The man sits for a moment in total silence, he hasn't moved an inch, seeming to look right through Enchantress. Spiderman is transfixed staring, he notices the hairs first. The hairs on Magneto's hands rise followed by a slight shaking, his skin seems to turn red as his whole body starts to resemble a volcano seconds before eruption. When he does erupt, boy does he erupt. Lots of things happen around the room instantaneously, Spiderman tries to take it all in, in one glorious beautiful terrifying moment, as Magneto stands his chair flies and shatters on the wall behind him, wall units and tables (in fact anything made of metal) either explodes or implodes with a deafening clatter. Magneto doesn't say a word, no, he roars, a wild uncontrollable ferocious roar with his head to the ceiling. Spiderman sits in his chair watching the whole beautiful eruption a huge smile and tears running down his weird red face, he watches Magneto finish his roar, watches him turn and storm his cape swooping and fluttering behind him as if it has its own mind. He sits there for a while in that hypnotic state you find yourself in when something extraordinary or breath-taking happens, but eventually breaking his reverie he stands and gives his head a slight shake. He sprints, swings and scuttles his way at lightning speed through the tunnels until he's in the control room and immediately deploys one of his mosquitos, he looks at the screens of the cave and is delighted to see Magneto only just zooming out on his disc looking even more menacing with thousands of tiny ball bearings buzzing around him, his own personal swarm of black glistening metal. Spiderman immediately tells the mosquito to watch Magneto, he takes his first drink in of the control room noticing that the other two assholes aren't here obsessing as usual over the fuckheads on the screens above him, but feels its time he should go find them and bring them up to speed, after all they are all in this together, so it's time they started to act like it.

The Manor 2009

H has taken over, it was Dave's brainwave but you know H, once you put an idea in the fuckers head it's there until it decomposes. The idea of course was chill out day, movies, guitars, food, and a fuckload of friendship splashed on top "am sortin everythin out before I start chillin and watchin movies an that, am gona bring all the guitars down an that, I'll even set guitar hero up for you before I go join Sup for a bit" that's what H had stated and that's what he did. Sid watches him fascinated, everything brought down in its place for the coming night, all laid out to perfection. Trudges off to the cinema giving the guys left in the room the finger "see ye later fuckedd's." Sid takes the last few pulls on his joint and stubs it out in the ashtray, looking at the stump as he crushes it, always feeling a little bit of remorse like he's just killed a close pet. He grabs his mug from the table only to be disappointed, the fuckers empty, he gets up in stoned robotic mode and heads for the kitchen where he knows H has a huge pot brewing nicely. As he walks to the kitchen he's in that trancey mood you sometimes find yourself in when you're so relaxed and without knowing it all your life experience and intuition are working full pelt, you see and feel things like Jason Bourne. Something registers in Sid's head and luckily he just lets it sink and settle, without really knowing it Sid enters the kitchen and grabs a brand new coffee, as he looks around he heads out and places it on the table "here ya go Brian lad, thought you moight like a fresh one, I'm just having a little mooch around the manor" he turns and goes to the gym room, has a little mess with a few of the weights a little look around and a few digs at the bags, he then slips outside having a good mooch around by the courts throwing a few balls at the baskets, he tries a few backward, he looks around the jacuzzi sitting on the side running his fingers through the water, he mooches through the library and the cinema having a real good look at all the books music and DVD's and then he heads into the games room, he's in here for ages to be honest having a go at everything in the room, pool, pinball and a good crack at space invaders. Sid heads out and up to his bedroom through all the hallways looking at all the pictures and décor and once he's finished in his own room he heads out and back down the hall to the toilet, he has a good gander as he has a shit and then it's onto the communal room. Sid plonks himself down on the plush mega comfy couch and rolls himself another joint, he puts a spark to that fat smelly fucker and grabs one of the guitars.

No 10 Downing street 2009

Kevin is bored fucking shitless, what a cunt, how the fuck do you end up with an asshole assignment like this, who the fuck did I piss off. He's been standing outside number ten downing street for seven hours straight and his legs are fucking killing, its not like there's any action going on here as well, it's been boring as fuck lately, no camera men no TV. He's wondering why he has to stand with his arms behind his back, how the fuck can I defend myself with my fucking arms behind my back. He glances without moving his head up the street to the left, fuckall happening there, he has a sly glance up the street to his right and can't believe it, fuckkall happening there just a weird swarm up over the trees. The swarm catches Kevin's attention to such a level that he completely forgets himself and moves slightly from his post, but to be fair on Kevin the swam is closing in on his direction. There's also something about the swarm that just isn't quite right, something in the centre that just doesn't make sense and fuck me its getting close coming straight for him. The swarm of metal balls suddenly streak forward at lightning speed to leave Magneto silently floating down on his metal disc. The swarm hits poor Steven and instantly turns him to a mushy pulp turning then and hitting the door of number ten and turning it into splinters. Magneto glides through all this carnage cape flapping in through the demolished door of number ten. He re-emerges moments later dragging Gordon Brown by the collar through the door looking like a schoolchild being dragged into the headmaster's office screaming and kicking. Magneto throws the prime minister of England into the street and glides out and up, his swarm growing gliding around him protecting him like a dark menacing phantom. Two of the jet-black cast iron metal bars suddenly detach themselves from the gates of number ten, they fly at the prime minister and wrap themselves around his wrists pulling him into the Jesus position. Gordon Brown is terrified, what the fuck is going on and who the fuck is Woooo, the bars wrap his wrists and within a split second pull him into the most agonising positions. The last thing the police see as they stream into downing street sirens blasting is the prime minister floating into the sky with a weird swarm of something beside him.

The Cave 2009.

Spiderman had run, crawl, fly whatever'd his way back through the tunnels and roused the other two, they had all sprinted to the control room crashing into it almost knocking each other over. Spiderman had brought them up to speed as they monitored the monitors, Ra's running Straight to Enchantress and Sabretooth busying himself with preparing the dungeons again. The mosquito had filled them in on Magnetos escapades and it's not long before the man himself comes floating into the room prime minister in toe limp and only held up by the bars around his wrists. Magneto drops him to the floor and without a word Sabretooth shoots forward and grabs the human dragging him off, Spiderman is immediately at Magnetos side filling him in on things, he can tell Magneto is still furious "we were awaiting you sire, Enchantress is good Ra's al Ghul is with her now tending her and Sabretooth has the dungeons at the ready" "good Spiderman, thank you, you are a true friend and good lieutenant your preparations are second to none for you guessed right, we go out tonight and take every important person in the Army and government in this shithole country, they're coming with us to the building we are pushing forward with our plans, I do not care any longer what state they are in we go ahead with our plans, how are the machines coming along?" "all the machines and preparations are up to speed boss I will have them taken to the building and put into position tonight but the monitors only tell us good things as time goes on, all they are is gross stoners boss, we could cut them down anytime" "good I am going to see her, make sure our guest is in extreme pain for the remainder of his stay." Magneto strides off leaving Spiderman dizzy with joy. He scuttles off to the dungeon to join Sabretooth and the new guest.

The Manor 2009.

H has just finished watching the third X Men movie, he stands up and does a fucking massive yawn "wwwhhhaaaaa fuckinell am stiff as fuck" Brodi and Blade join H in the stretching but Superman's up and straight over to the stack of DVD's to load in his next movie "fuckinell Sup lad" shouts Blade "yow not goin to give it a minute" Superman doesn't even turn "I have too many movies to catch up on my friend, next up is you, The Blade Trilogy are you not going to join me?" "sorry Sup lad but I've seen them too many times" "yer me too mate I'm off for a bit of the old guitar mush" says H. just then Sid enters the cinema and comes over mooching around the cinema "now then lads just thought I'd pop in while there's a break on have a look around an that, I haven't really been in ere yet" "well knock yeself out mush we're off to the communal room for a few joints and that, you comin Bri?" "I lads, I could do with a break like, three fucking movies in a row like, haven'y done that for a while am fooked" the guys pile out as Superman gets himself comfy again, in fact he's so comfortable he doesn't even know Sid is next to him until the sweet weed aroma hits his nostrils, he turns to Sid smiling "arrrr splendid Sid I'd run out."

Back in the communal room and its joints flowing drinks sloshing, not anything like the previous night though just a nice chilled out atmosphere as the lad's pile in and grab the guitars. H on the other had had realised as he came out of the cinema that he was starving heads to the kitchen to put in some quick bites as he finds menus for the local restaurants and takeaway. He brings in a tray of colds and cheeses as he asks the gang in turn what they would like "ye can order anything guys, there's fuckin everthin, Italian, Indian, Chinese, English the fuckin lot. H goes around until he's got the lot "I betta go and ask the lads in the cine do they want anything" H flies off to the cinema as the gang tuck into the fiddles. Brian has the guitar and is doing a bit of fingerpicking "arr I fuckin love that song Bri" Says Mel "it's Moby right" "yer love, Ever-loving it's fuckin groyt init" he caries on picking and humming. Blade sitting next to him hums along as he builds a joint but his eyes are on the empty Wii remote sitting on the floor next to Dave, Lysa and Emma who are furiously battling it out on Mario Kart. Dave's kicking ass and to be fair so he fucking should with the fucker never being off it. Blade finishes rolling his joint and dives down on the carpet grabbing the remote but the race is still ongoing, he dives in with a bit of banter to let the guys know there's a new contender "Davy boy here been kickin yow asses girls, well it's game on in the next race fuckers I'm the fuckin Mario fuckin master" all three are giggling trying not to lose concentration "shat the fock up bollocks we'll see how good yer are in a minute" taunts Emma. H comes back in from the cine room and asks one more time before he orders "right has everyone deffo ordered everythin thy want cos I'm phonin now" all the gang shouting yer in unison and H is giving them the beady eye, he can see their not really listening but to be fair there's enough food to feed an army on the order so he hits the blower, he's got five different places to phone so it's going to take a while, Mel shouts over "oy H did the lads in the cine want anything" "fuckinell girl you better believe it, there's only two of them and they nearly ordered more than all you cunts" the gang are pissing it even the ones glued to the TV, you can see their shoulders shaking. H is straight on the phone and not before long there's a line of cars outside with the food. H scarpers to the cine all guns blazing to make sure the guys come, he storms through the doors and flicks the lights blaringly bright "come on you pair o cunts yer not stayin in here and eatin" he walks straight through and pauses the movie "you could do with a rest anyhow Sup yer fuckin eyes are all fuckin red" the two guys eventually relent laughing with H "come on lads you don't want to be too antisocial do ye" the guys head out just in time as the feast has been laid out and looks fucking amazing, every food of every kind near enough. The gang all tuck in as the night gets off to a cracker, the next thing you know there's joints flowing drinks, a game of Wii sports is on the go with everybody screaming. The guitars come out and it's fucking acoustic night, you better believe it, some crackers get smashed out on them guitars, Jose Gonzales, Clash, Led Zep, fucking loads from Led Zep 3, the Floyd of course, Johnny Cash, James Morrison and fucking Jim and the Doors, Joy Division, good few of The Beatles, The Stones, bit of Metallica, Pearl Jam, Radiohead, Stained, some cunt even does a James Blunt number, o yes the list goes on my friends as does the night. Superman had gone back to the cinema after an hour or so but to be fair nobody else wanted to leave the fun, the game of Wii Sports is well over and they've done Wii fit and now they're onto the brand-new Wii Sports Resort. The night couldn't get any better the banters flowing joints burning, H and Brian are neck and neck in a game of archery that had well pissed off Dave because the soft cunt actually goes to a real archery range and Brian keep winding him up "ye canny be much of an archer like Dave lad, me and H fuckun battad ye" "fuckoff bollocks it's not real life" shouts Dave as wham H wins with a whisker "fuckin get in there you fuckin beauty, I AM THE CHAMPION MY FRIENDS" H is singing hands in the air and Brian's looking at him well pissed,

Dave's laughing pointing at Brian made up that he's getting his own back that is until Brian the stupid fucker bites and like the cunt he is sending the night into chaos "fuck you H" he springs his middle blade out showing it to H's face "at least I can still Wolverine up like, ya fuckin human, all you can do now soft-ass is Hulk your dick out arrrr, ha, ha, ha,… Brian goes off in a mad fit of laughter, but there's only Brian laughing. The room goes deathly silent, everybody except Brian looking at H with, well, awkward looks on their faces really, Brian's still laughing, kind of circling looking at everyone for support but as his eyes meet more and more faces he realises he's fucked up and his laugh embarrassingly dies down. H has gone beetroot red and Dave's deathly white as he looks at his friend with a pained look spreading across his kipper "fuckin nice one MATE!" says H vehemently. Dave's panicking "H I didn't mean it H, I was stoned kid, it just slipped out… a… a… H honest, me and Brian were gabbing and…" H is having none of it, he's fucking fuming "well, tell them somthin about yer-fuckin-self next time" H storms off in the direction of the stairs and Lysa jumps up to run after him, the rest of the guys are looking at each other all awkward like. Mel does a big fake yawn "arrrr I'm fuckin knackerd, think I'll knock a few joints up and go watch a bit of a movie with Sup before bed" she couches down and starts with her rolling as the rest of the gang are still all looking uncomfortable. Brian's gutted and turns to Dave "arrrr Davey man I didn'y mean it like, am sorry like Dave, I forgot you said and…" Dave just shrugs his shoulders "it's all right Bri don't worry about it mush, we've been through this loads of times, he'll calm down later, it'll be fine, just let him cool off, Lysa u'll sort him out, he'll be fine, just crack on with yer night guys don't let it spoil yer fun." This little cooling session of words from Dave does smooth things out a little and the guys start to relax. Brodi and Emma start a new game on the Wii and Sid grabs a pad. Blade, just finishing a joint, pops it in his mouth and grabs one of the guitars, he starts plucking I'm One by the Who and even Mel looks up when Blade starts singing; big smile beaming at Blade and joining in "every year is the same and I feel it again I'm a loser, no chance to win" this relaxes the guys a little more and even Brian takes a pew. He plonks himself down next to Dave all apologetic again "I really am sorry Dave I..." Dave holds his palm out to Brian's face "Brian chill the fuck out mush it's fine" Brian looks a bit gutted for a second as Dave was rather curt, but a huge grin spreads across Dave's his kipper as he flicks his hand and a joint appears out of thin air "go on mush spark this bad-boy up.

The Cave 2009.

When Magneto entered the sick ward, Ra's looked up and smiled at his old friend, he noticed the strain or worry on his face for the first time in years. Magneto lays his hand on Enchantress's head "she looks peaceful, how is she? Has she stirred again?" "no, my friend she has been like this for hours." A chair slides from somewhere in the room and stops behind Magneto and he sits, the whole movement one flowing beautiful dance. Ra's watches him for a while before getting up, he pats his friend on the back letting him know that he's there "I will leave you alone for a while, call if you need anything" "I will be fine, I have told Spiderman what needs done" Ra's sets off through the caves to the control room. He checks the monitors and spots Sabretooth and Spiderman in the dungeons and heads down. He finds the guys arguing over how far to go with the torture of the prime minister, obviously Spiderman wanting more "come you two, leave the human we have lots to do tonight, Spiderman what did Magneto request for tonight" "first we load the van with the machines, they need taking to the building and setting up, then we have lots of humans to visit, I'll get the addresses while you two take the machines to the building, I'll meet you there to set them up" "good Spiderman good, you have done well my friend" Ra's pats Spiderman as they set off up the stairs, Spiderman and Sabretooth seeming to forget their differences in the light of the recent happenings. They head for the room where Spiderman had been putting the machines once they were working and commence to load them into a van. The last one just being packed and Spiderman remembers "There is one more in my room, come Sabretooth bring the trolley" when they enter Spiderman's room the first thing they see is the human webbed to the wall "who and what the fuck is that?" asks Ra's with an arm out finger pointing for total emphasis, "it is the human surgeon that Magneto brought to mend Enchantress, he was snooping around, so..." "Sabretooth and I will load this last one, take him down with the other and then carry on with your duties" Spiderman is livid, the human was his, he found him, or rather the other way round really, and who the fuck was he, Ra's al Ghul, who the fuck did he think he was, Magneto had given me the orders to give out not this fucking ass. Spiderman bites his tongue for now and nods his assent.

The Building 2009

Sabretooth and Ra's enter the building and have a good mooch about "wow, it is as he said, a magnificent building, this will do pleasantly" the two men look at what Magneto had already been doing and carry on bringing in the new contraptions and getting things ready. When all is done the two men stand back admiring their work "do you really think we will go along with this plan, kidnaping and killing people?" asks Sabretooth looking at Ra's with doubt and fear in his eyes "I do not know my friend but with what has come to pass recently with enchantress, god only knows what will happen, but we must stand together, we have been family for a long time Sabretooth, now may not be the time for abandoning our friends, whatever our hearts tell us, we shall just have to wait and see how things pan out."

The Cave 2009.

The van drives toward the humongous metal doors, they look like something from a UFO movie, a jet would look like a toy next to them, set into the rock and virtually invisible until you come right up onto them, wheels popping on the rough stone path the van comes to a stop and the doors slowly rise. As the doors rise the silhouette or shadow of Spiderman creeps out along the floor toward the van. The two men look at each shaking their heads contempt on their faces as the doors rise and the full figure of Spiderman standing on the loading bay hands on hips comes into view, the van chugs into the bay as Spiderman comes running to the van. "quickly, Magneto wants us immediately, she has woken" he scuttles off and the two men look at each other not knowing whether to be excited or worried, they run for the sick bay room. As they enter they see Magneto tending to Enchantress, he holds a glass of water tipping it delicately. Enchantress lies on the bed awake now but looking week sipping the water offered by Magneto. Spiderman has already taken a seat as the two men approach the bed and take seats of their own. The four men sit looking at Enchantress and eventually she stirs again eyes fluttering as she struggles for consciousness, she tries to sit up but can't. "do not stress yourself my dear, rest" "shut up man" she retorts "and help me sit up" Magneto looking embarrassed lifts her slightly up onto the pillows, she lies back smiling looking at the men. Tell us what has happened to you asks Ra's, who did this to you? "I... I was looking for the Marvellous," her voice throaty and rough, Magneto tries to give her more water but she pushes it away "I had heard rumours that the government knew about them, maybe even had one or two of them, but alas, I fear it was all a trap, lured I was, I was told of a secret facility deep in the hills of the Lake District, so I travelled to Coniston and under the Old Man found a huge city, a government and army facility. I had sneaked in through the walls or so I thought, but they knew, they knew my powers," she grabs Magneto "I don't know how they did it but I was surrounded, they put some kind of devise around my neck, powerless I was dragged down long tunnels" she looks to the men with fear and fury in her eyes "I saw others, men and women we thought dead long ago, Darkseid, Harley, and Rorschach I saw all being horrendously tortured, I do not even know if they were alive. They kept me there for months taking blood, DNA and any other bodily fluid the could extract" she bursts into tears but then roars "they even tried to inseminate me, tried to get me pregnant, they were saying they could make their own, fucking dirty fucki..." Magneto bubbles with rage you can almost see it emanating from his pores "they will all die for this, we will kill them all, this facility is the starting place" he turns to Spiderman "go now and take those humans I have asked for, take Sabretooth with you I want them all here when I return, and tonight you will go to the manor, bring that big green piece of shit to the building for it begins now. Magneto strides away as One tiny metal boll Bering floats toward him it flattens to a disc as it approaches and lands on the floor, Magneto steps on in one beautiful fluid movement and the disc swoops him off through the doors. He screams at speed through the tunnels and out through the huge doors left open by the two men out and up into the sky. He thunders a lightning speed toward the Lake District. He spots the Old Man as he thunders onward knowing it instantly for its famous tarns and swoops down looking for an entrance. These men, human men had done a good job for nowhere could an entrance be sought. Magneto swoops down into an old abandoned tunnel, old rail tracks lifting and ripping up behind him blocking the way, the earth shakes and shifts around him as a huge rip appears in the wall, a huge seam of metal in the rock melting and forming into his desired tools until boom the rock explodes into a huge tunnel. There where men waiting in the humongous tunnel soldiers and heavily armoured Humvee; all lasted only seconds, Magneto crushes the three Humvee with the men inside screaming, the trucks made so small seeming to defy the laws of physics to just little metal cubs on the floor with blood seeping out. The hundreds if not thousands of bullets that had exploded from the guns and rifles and semi-automatics stop millimetres from Magneto. He stands smiling now looking at the men who are now shiting themselves; they were told this might happen told somebody might come but… Magneto turns the bullets into his favourite little eddy and again the men watching mesmerised as the bullets start to swirl, but the mesmerisation only lasts for a few seconds as the bullets soon roar and rip into the screaming men turning them to mush. Magneto heads of down the huge tunnel looking for some sort of control room, he spies a man trying to run and sends one of his balls over, the metal ball flattens out and wraps itself around the mans arm bringing him to Magneto "where is the control room with the monitors" the man looking terrified tries to draw up a last grasp at defiance "I'm tellin you fuck all dickedd" but Magneto just laughs "that my friend I think not" the metal on the mans arm suddenly turns to liquid and starts to travel all over the mans body probing and seeping into crevices the man never knew he had, two veins creep up the mans face and tiny pinpricks threaten the man's eyes as another two creep into his ears probing, hurting, more liquid seeps around his fingernails. The last straw comes when the man feels the metal on his penis slithering around his testicles squeezing and then probing his bell-end, as the metal seeps up into his penis the man relents "OK… ok whatever you want man, whatever you want. The man takes Magneto to the monitor room, Magneto killing whatever comes at him on the way "stupid humans covering themselves with metals thinking they are precious; why not cover yourself with stones off the floor. As more and more soldiers try and attack Magneto they are killed by their own trinkets as fingers fall to the floor severed by rings. Arms, hands and legs fall as precious bracelets tear them apart, earrings rip from ears, nipple rings and nose rings; they all betray the owner. The worst are the necklaces severing heads, religious saints once the protectors suddenly turn on their owner dropping his head to the floor. Magneto pays no mind to the madness as he glides through and once in the control room he sees the full spectrum of the fortress he's infiltrated. Most of the humans are dead with others he can see alerting other military bases or whoever for help, let them come he thinks, let them come. He spies the cells or rather the glass boxes holding the other prisoners that Enchantress had told them about. Magneto can't tell from the moniters if the prisoners are dead or alive so decides to see for himself walking out of the control room as it implodes behind him tearing his guide to shreds. Magneto glides down a long tunnel toward a huge football-stadium sized room slicing and splattering anything in his way. The room had been split up into divisions of labs and medical rooms but still open-plan, Magneto glides through on his disc toward the glass boxes. He goes to them opening them up; Darkseid being the only one dead he makes metal cocoons from the gleaming stainless tables and wraps the other two up. As he floats out of the room; cocoons out in front the room behind him erupts and explodes. Magneto glides back through the tunnels, cocoons out front to the opening that he came in from, as he glides upward' he spies two military chinooks coming toward him. Magneto laughs as he turns the two chinooks to liquid watching the men and bits of plastic and none metal drop hundreds of feet to the rocky mountain far below.

The Cave 2009.

Spiderman and Sabretooth pull up into the loading bay; Ra's al Ghul stands waiting, listening to the moaning, gasping pleas from the van. The two men (well, one man; the other hasn't got a dick) exit the van and start to lower the tailgate revealing the cattle-packed humans inside. There're about fifty humans packed into the back of the pickup truck, it looks like a horrendous news scene about people trafficking as they pile out falling over each other; Ra's starts screaming at the humans "in line, filthy beasts" there's women crying and screaming, men crying and moaning as Ra's files them in. Sabretooth pats Ra's on the shoulder and nods to the sky behind them; a figure can be seen returning. "Here comes Magneto get these filthy animals out of his way to the dungeon" the two cocoons precede Magneto to the bay; he lands moments later in the middle of them "where is my surgeon I brought earlier, these two are in need of him urgently" if Spiderman's face could turn red, but it already was; he stammers "I... I have him downstairs for you boss, I will fetch him immediately" Ra's gives Spiderman a condescending look as he scuttles of whipping the humans down with him. "Spiderman" shouts Magneto before he can disappear "I want you to go to the manor tonight, take Sabretooth with you, the plan starts tonight, you know what to do" Sabretooth and Ra's have a quick sly glance at each other not knowing what was going on but carry one when nothing more is said, Spiderman scuttles back off with a sly smile creeping across his face. "Ra's, come with me we need to see how badly wounded they are" Magneto strides into the cave the two cocoons floating ahead. When they enter the now more permanent surgery enchantress sits up awkwardly trying to see the newcomers. The cocoons stop and gracefully melt down transforming back into tables with Harley and Rorschach lying bloody and beaten. Ra's starts to strip them ready for the surgeon and also to see the extent of their injuries and not before long Spiderman comes in dragging the beat-up surgeon. Magneto explodes "what the fuck has happened to him" "I am sorry boss but I caught him earlier trying to escape, I did not know he was important" Magneto is livid "FUCKING IDIOT, Ra's al Ghul tend to the surgeon for me please and then get him to work on these two, I am going out to find another" Spiderman comes to Magneto's side grovelling "please boss let me go for you, I will bring bac..." "shut up and carry on with the chores you already have, and DO NOT! fuck up tonight Spiderman" Magneto storms from the room, cloak flapping all over the place like Batman. Spiderman is livid, being berated in front of these two is bad enough but being in the boss's bad books was the ultimate low, he knew he should have sent his little mosquito after him, stupid, stupid, stupid he thinks as he speeds as fast as possible toward his room, from now on my mosquitos go everywhere they follow everyone.

The Manor 2009.

The night has been cracking on famously, apart from the earlier little skirmish all's been good, it's getting pretty late now and most have retired to whatever night time activities they've chosen. Emma and Brodi had played on the Wii until late and then gone up for some fun and frolics. Mel as promised had gone to the cinema to watch a few movies with Superman. Dave, Blade and Sid had been alternating between playing Wii, playing guitars and building joints, but had eventually sloped off themselves, Blade joining the cinema goers and Dave and Sid retiring to their rooms, Dave popping the PlayStation on and smashing it out with Burnout, he's had enough of that now though and has settled down for the night with a bit of Killzone 2. Further down the hall, Sid, lying on his bed, big massive joint in his mouth has put the Black Keys on his mp3 player, they're one of his favourite groups ever he can't wait for their next album, he's listening with his brand new Beats by Dre headphones; they've only just come out and cost a few bob but to be fair they're the fucking shit, his music has never sounded so immense, he's hearing things he never heard before, he decides he's deffo buying everyone a pair for Chrimbo, if they're still here that is. He's doing something really tricky and intricate on his laptop and can't believe what he's seeing.

H and Lysa had gone to H's room after the bust up, Lysa quaking at first thinking that H would be fuming or pissed but H was fine; said he was a little embarrassed in front of the gang that's all, and after a few joints and a little tipple they spend the rest of the evening throwing themselves all over the room. Time has now ticked on and the pair of them are fast asleep having put on Kill Bill volumes one and two, the second movie still playing on the huge TV Uma on her way to Bills house for the final showdown. Outside and directly below Spiderman and Sabretooth stand looking up at the window "wait here, I will call you when I'm ready" Spiderman lowers his headphones from his head to his ears; he takes out his mp3 player scanning for the perfect tune; he's thinking of his usual, Lullaby by The Cure, but tonight fancies something more evil, he spies the perfect tune and taps the play button and the beautiful eerie amalgam of instruments and sound hits his ears as Radiohead's Little by Little pour from the player. O how he loves this song the perfect soundtrack for the night's activities creepy and evil. Spiderman hits the wall and starts that creepy crawl up the side of the building and even Sabretooth has to look away disgusted at the sight. Spiderman crawls on reaching the window peeking in at the two sleeping lovebirds. He takes out his mini cordless drill and pilots a tiny hole in the wooden frame of the window. He takes out a canister and tube; inserting the tube into the tiny hole and fixing it to the canister. He pushes the button and watches the noxious green gas escape from the canister and flow into the bedroom. He lets the gas do its job for a few minutes before taking out a small remote device and clicking a button; suddenly the window to the room starts to rise as green gas escapes from the room to the night sky. He takes the rope ladder from his satchel and attaches it to the window allowing Sabretooth to make the climb. When Sabretooth nears the top Spiderman passes him a mask "there may still be gasses left over and trust me my friend you do not want to inhale them" Sabretooth puts on the mask and enters the room wrapping up H in a huge blanket and taking him out first; climbing down and resting H on the grass and then returning for Lysa. Sabretooth is momentarily spellbound by the sight of Lysa asleep naked in the bed, lithe body, amazing full round breasts, his eyes drift down to her WoW, a twang of fear, excitement, and seedy guilt hits Sabretooth as he looks at Lysa's amazing pussy, shaven bald and throbbing after the hammering that H had given it. Sabretooth apart from a few pornos hadn't seen a real pussy up close like this before and as I said the fuckers mesmerised "stop perving and rap her up, we haven't got time for this shit" Spiderman breaks his reverie "fuckoff no dick; you have NO idea." Sabretooth rolls raps and swoops Lysa up in one fluid movement, he moves to the window leaving Spiderman to tidy things up like nothing untoward had ever happened. Spiderman tidy's the room and takes a few things to make it look like H had gone off somewhere. He's thinking about going to Lysa's room to do the same but in two minds, he pops out a little monitor and checks the cameras in the house; he decides to risk it. He scuttles down the hall and into Lysa's room taking a few things and leaving draws open, making it look like she left in a hurry. He checks his monitors again and all's clear, he opens the door scuttling off down the hall and just as he thinks he's home free the door to Dave's room opens suddenly in front of him. He freezes and for a Nano second closes his eyes expecting when they open to see the startled face of Mr Fantastic; instead its Dave's cock slithering out of the door on its way to the toilet, and Spiderman could swear it was looking at him with its one beady eye. He dives around Dave's dick and scuttles back off to H's room and out of the window closing up and removing the ladder. Sabretooth is waiting in the van "fuck have you been up to, I've been waiting here ages" Spiderman gives Sabretooth the nastiest condescending look he's ever given as he gets comfortable in his seat he then turns and looks straight forward "some of us are important my friend, we are important because we are useful and can operate without being told what to do, every second of every day, we have ideas of our own my friend and make the group stronger, plus, we never fuck up" he turns now and looks again at Sabretooth "and some of us are just useless fucking planks my friend. Now hurry, they will be waiting" Sabretooth turns giving the same look right back "arrrr, then you obviously thought on and have one of their sets of car keys in your pocket, and you don't really want to get in this truck with me because you will be driving one of their cars, or I could be wrong being a fucking plank" Spiderman fuming, climbs from the van and storms back off to try find keys, the fucking prick was right, why hadn't he thought of it, stupid, stupid, stupid. He heads back and re-enters the manor the same way and finds the keys pretty quick then he's back down and round to the cars. He clicks the keys and the Audi RS Spider's lights flash and he's in, WOW fucking beautiful he's thinking as he drinks in the plush hand stitched seats and interior. This should be mine anyhow it's a fucking spider. He fires the bitch up and roars out, the only consolation is when he flies past Sabretooth chugging along in his shit slow wagon.

The Cave 2009.

The van pulls up to the humongous doors of the loading bay, the Audi already parked up in the pitch-dark night and suddenly BOOM, floodlights burst on lighting the bay like a football stadium. The prize in the back of the van is so important that even Enchantress has come down to look, wheelchair and all. Sabretooth climbs from the back and lowers the gate. Spiderman, Sabretooth, Magneto, Enchantress and Ra's al Ghul all stand in the back of the van looking down at the sleeping figures of Hulk and Mystique. Its Magneto that breaks the silence, he scoffs first "how easy it would be, we could kill them now and have it done with" there's silence again for a while as they drink this in "but what fun would that be my friends, what fun would that be" Magneto turns and strides from the van "Spiderman carry on with the plans, take them to the building and strap them to their new devices, leave taking the humans until tomorrow." Ra's grabs Enchantress's chair and turns, Sabretooth falls in beside him "how are the other two? Have they come around yet?" "no, my friend they have not woken but the two surgeons are hard at work on them as we speak they are much mended, now go and do as the master asks Sabretooth." Sabretooth stand for a while watching them disappear down the cave tunnel before returning to the van for a long boring night.

The Manor 2009.

Mel wakes up in the cinema with a mouth like a camels ass-hole "aw fuck me I feel rough" she looks over at Superman and Blade who are still engrossed in movies "fuck me guys are you still watchin these fuckin movies ye must av seen every fuckin superhero movie ever made" Blade starts laughing "not yet babe, there's fuckin hundreds" Mel does a huge stretch "aaaaaaaaaaarrrrrrrrrrrr fuck-in-hell that was nice, think I'm gona get some breaky lads, you want me to fetch ye some in" the two men for the first time drag their eyes from the screen "OOO YES Mel fuckin lovely." Mel dives up and makes her way to the kitchen; as she walks in, she spots Dave sitting at the table looking all sorry for himself "fuckinell Dave you all right babe" "yer, just... I went in to see H the smornin and he's gone" he looks up and smiles "his cars gone as well, he's done it before like, fucks off all the time surfin an that, but I just wanted to see if he was sound an that" Mel don't half feel sorry for Dave, she gives him the puppy dog eyes for a bit of support "he'll be cool Dave love, an yer he's probably skating I'll pop up and see Lysa an ask her where he's gone" " nice one Mel love I'll pop the breaky on while ye gone." Dave jumps up and starts with the breakfast and Mel heads up to Lysa's room. On her way up, she passes Sid "mornin Sid I'll be back down in a sec I'm just goin to see Lysa" "no probs Mel and mornin love." Sid heads into the kitchen and joins Dave making the breakfast saying their good mornings. They chat for a while, Dave telling Sid about H being gone and Sid agreeing that he's somewhere up to no good. Mel comes back in with Brodi and Emma "Lysa's not in her room either, there's things gone and it looks like she left in a hurry, her an H must have fucked off somewhere for a bit" Brodi's a bit suspicious though "bit strange though don't you think, the two of them just up and leave without saying anything to anybody" Sid dives in and says he thinks he did hear them last night messing around on the landing. The gang take this in and chat a bit more as they all chip in making breakfast going over the previous night and agreeing that they've probably just gone out for the day. Sid excuses himself saying he wants to go see the lads in the cinema "they're gona come eat breakfast in err with the rest of us, they're not sitting in there eating like fuckin animals." He jogs off laughing and this sets a better scene in the kitchen as its smiles all round, and this sets Dave off telling jokes and fucking about with the girls. Sid bounces into the cinema and takes a seat next to blade and after saying hello and settling in for a few minutes in his chair he turns invisible. He comes up right in the middle of Superman and Blade "we're going on a day out today boys cos there's trouble afoot, when we bring it up in the kitchen just go along with it." Sid then goes on a little invisible walk, he slips through the door and into the kitchen, he slides up to Dave first trying not to startle him and whispers the same. What happens next is quite comical if you were sitting at the table when Sid goes around the gang one by one, the sudden jerky head, Mel even did a little yelp and had to quickly make an excuse. Once Sid is finished the sneaky fucker sets off back to the cinema, he takes his seat and a few minutes later starts to berate the lads about not being at breakfast and makes a big show of dragging them to the kitchen. Once all the gang are assembled and eating away, chatting shit, the usual, Sid starts to voice his secret plan "anyone fancy a day out today, we've been cooped up in this place for days, I could do with a breather, no wonder H and Lysa fucked off, this place is cool but it's getting to be like a coffin" "what ye wanna do then Sid?" "I duno to be fair ladies and gents anyone got any suggestions" Dave buts in "fuckin right, I know where we're goin, the fuckin Chill Factor in Manchester, it's fuckin boss, best day out ever, apart from Alton Towers like" his little face lights up as he looks around the faces "come on guys who doesn't love a bit of skiin or snowboarding" "err" Superman buts in looking worried "I have never actually skied or snowboarded, whatever that is" the whole gang look from one to another; grins spreading across their faces and in one glorious choir "the fuckin Chill Factor it is." Dave takes over as the spearhead of the mission "right Sid you get on the dit-dot-com and get everyone booked in, am not avin any messin when we get there, I wana be all booked in, straight in, right gang here's a list of stuff ye gona need." Everyone sets off on their own little missions to get the day under way and not before long there's a little group loitering by the front door ready and waiting to go. Dave lends Superman some of his clothes with them being near the same size, the two girls are delighted "wit woo look at you" Superman's all blushes as he heads out the front door. Brodi wants to go in Emma's Bugatti and Brian says that he'll take Dave and Superman so Sid Blade and Mel decide to all go in Sid's X6. "foockin loveloy this Sid" says Blade as they climb in, Sid keeps clocking the sky as he gets himself ready. Dave shouts shotgun as they go to Brian's car but it doesn't really mater with Superman not having a fucking clue what Dave's going on about, so Dave just walks and gets in the front. As he climbs in he's shocked as there's six massive slashes or stabs in the beautiful leather dash of the Austin Martin "fuck me Bri, what the fuck append to ye car?" Brian looks at the slashes shaking his head "arrrr don't fuckin ask Davey lad, don't fuckin ask." Dave shrugs as he slides into the seat and the three cars pull slowly off the drive.

The Building 2009.

Magneto lands on the roof of the building and walks to the parapet. He stands looking down into the town; watching the humans about their day. Soon you will all pay he's thinking, soon you will all suffer, in fact, he thinks about releasing another set of ball-bearings but then thinks twice about it as it may attract unwanted attention. He walks away across the roof to the door down into the building to see how the plans are coming along. The others have been busy most of the night and were up early; they had all left the cave together for this journey, Spiderman coming in is new Audi leaving Ra's and

Sabretooth in the truck; Magneto wanting to see how the building looked now with everybody there. They had left enchantress back at the cave watching over the doctors and keeping an eye on the monitors but Spiderman (sneaky little fucker that he is) has his little screens and devices to keep us in the loop. He walks into the room and is not disappointed, the guys have done an amazing job. Hulk and Mystique where over on the right, the Hulk shackled with humongous wrist and ankle straps made metal, but Mystique just tied and gagged. Both had been sedated and left under until Magneto said it was time. The centre of the floor (probably the dance floor) had been left empty but all around it where the people that had been kidnaped; they were gagged and chained to a metal balustrade circling the centre. There was another device on the right that was empty and all the little surprises had also been rigged "SPLENDID, SPLENDID, you have done wonders my friends" Magneto walks down along the levels of the old building toward the centre, the men looking up from their chores smiling. Spiderman creeps over to have a little grovel "boss, everything is as you wanted, these two will be out until you say otherwise" "good, and nice touch with the captives tying them there, they look good, sets the mood wouldn't you say" "thank you boss we thought you would like that" "and what of the others do they suspect anything?" "no boss I have been watching the monitors, everything is fine, they think these two here have gone out together for the day, they have gone out themselves" "THEMSELVES" Magneto looks at Spiderman fury in his eyes "master it is fine, they have gone skiing for the day to relax but I have my little spy's watching them." He holds his webbed hand up in surrender but Magnetos face relaxes as he nods "ok, ok, but keep your eye on them I want this to go perfectly, the day after tomorrow maybe." Magneto walks down away from Spiderman to the captives and Spiderman goes back to his duties with Sabretooth and Ra's, listening to the howls and pleas from below.

The Chill Factor 2009

The gang come off the motorway into the tangle of roundabouts that leads to the Chill Factor, they glide into the carpark and it's all eyes on them as the three cars purr in and park alongside each other. The guys all pile out and laugh and joke their way in. they stop at a few shops in the foyer and do a little bit of shopping, and Superman gets rigged out to the max by the gang; Dave even buys him a snowboard. They have a little snack just to fill themselves just before the fun begins, but Sid always scanning the surroundings. As most of the gang have been here before they blag Superman in and its off to the snow, all of them have decided to snowboard which is probably best for Superman as they have to hold him most of the time but they're having the time of their lives laughing and showing off. The guys go all out against each other and start to do some crazy aerial tricks until they get told off. After they've been there a few hours Sid spots Superman a watches him for a minute, he was getting quite good after being thrown in at the deep end, but Sid can see that he's about to go tits up and glides in beside him just as he does; Sid's laughing his ass off "come on Sup lad yer gettin quite good" as Sid bends down and hug Superman to help him up he whispers "I think there's somthin watchin us Sup, Somthin small, sort it out big man" he carries on lifting Superman and laughing patting him down, as Sid does this Superman with his love for his new found friends moves so fast and with so much passion that time itself almost stops, he scans the room and spots the tiny mosquito watching the gang. Superman sends a ray from his eyes and hits the bug and all this without even a second gone by "it is done Sid we are no longer being watched" Sid is blinking looking bewildered "fuck me Sup that was quick, wot was it?" "a tiny fly or something like a fly with a microscopic camera" "yer thought they would have a camera watchin us" Superman grabs Sid "Sid who is they?" Sid smiles "come on Sup lad lets get the others and av a little chat, I don't think H and Lysa have gone mate, I think they've been taken" Superman's eyes fly wide open "I fucking knew it, come Sid." Superman and Sid snowboard to the bottom and wait for the others to come down rounding everyone up "come on gang lets go for a nose-bag, we've got a few things to talk about" the gang all head out changing and heading for the nearest diner "let's not eat here guys just in case, we'll go across to the Trafford centre to the massive food court" the gang are all looking quizzical at Sid "Sid what are you on about mate?" asks Mel "not now Mel love lets get over and get ourselves comfy in a little restaurant." The gang all clime back into their cars and head over to the food court choosing a little restaurant with a dark back booth; they all crowd in. the whole gang is assembled in the booth looking at each other tension and excitement building in the air. Sid looks around the faces and it's all eyes on Sid the whole gang looking at him eager; Sid opens his mouth; the gang lean in and the waiter appears "hi guys, and what would you like to drink" the gang burst out laughing to the bewilderment of the waiter as they give their order. Once the waiter had gone the gang jump on Sid like a pack o wolves "come on Sid what the fucks goin on" Sid takes a huge breath "right, the other day I wos sittin there stoned jus stairin at the ceilin when I spots something strange, now I wont go into it but I know a fair bit about gadgets and tech so curiosity gets the better of me and sure enough I was right" the gang are all looking from one to the other shrugging "the house was rigged guys with cameras and mics, every fackin room" the girls scream and the guys eyes nearly pop from their heads as the chorus of fuck off's and no fucking way's circulates for about a minute, the gang thinking of all the things they've been getting up to together and alone. "Sorry guys but it's true, every room all outside the carpark everywhere and mics, so I notice that in the cine there was only one cam and that's why I knew they wouldn't see me." Mel buts in first as the gang swarm on Sid with a thousand questions "did you find out who it is" "no Mel, whoever set the system up knows their stuff I tell ya, I couldn't break it for shit, all I could do was break into the cams in the house." Dave breaks in next worried for H "so ye don't know where they've taken H then" "no Dave I don't sorry" "am fuckin gutted gang here's me thinkin me mucka's gone off to cool down with his new bird an all along he's been fuckin kidnaped, I feel a right cunt" all the gang pile in on Dave to cheer him up telling him it wasn't his fault and that they were all to blame. "Right then shouts Emma who the fuck is doing this? why have they been watching us? and what the fuck do they want? And who's next on the list?" Dave jumps in "no fuck that, we're not goin back there we're fuckin findin out where H and Lysa are an we're goin getting them" he looks around the table at each of them, they all nod their assent in return. The last person Dave's eyes land on is Sid and Dave's in full flow "right Sid I've got a plan, the cheeky cunts robbed his car and the fuckin dozy cunts might still have it" "Dave you fuckin diamond, I neva thought of that, but I need all his info mate" "don't you fuckin worry mush, I was like the wife in our relationship, H thought every fuckin thing was free, I paid all the fuckin bills, I know all the shit mush." All the gang crowd in as Sid gets to work on the laptop and in no time at all like in the movies Sid comes up with the goodies. "Roight, the car went to two different places, first after leavin here it went fuckin miles mate, right out remote like with fuck all there, then it went to the city, av looked at the address and it's a big old warehouse, probably an old club or sumfin, then it's been goin there and back ever since, I can look see if there's any CCTV cameras nearby" Sid gets to work again and the gang seem to crowd in even more nattering away about who they think it is and what they're going to do to them when they find out. "Roight guys av got a few feeds but yer not gona like it" Sid swivels the laptop round so everyone can see. On the screen the usual grainy CCTV footage of a street, across the road you can see the club and the goings on in fast time-lapse mode, all you can here from the gang are gasps as they watch the footage of enemies from the past coming and going about their business, there's a grainy night time bit where you can just about make out figures being brought in. "O my fuckin god, we've gorra get down there now" shouts Dave, Superman puts his hand on Dave's arm "Dave my friend they have powers, great powers, that was Magneto you just saw, one of the most powerful beings on this earth" "ok, ok, so what do we do then Sup?" Superman starts to think out loud and the gang join in theorising the outcome of events and how to stop them. As they gab and chatter Blade mentions that it would solve everything if H could Hulk out and Dave goes off into his own little world for a while as the others gab on. Sid's telling everyone that he thinks there all in the building from the footage but Superman is saying that they should check the other place first because they know who and what is in the building but god only know what is at the other place. Dave buts in "guys I think I've got a plan" he points at Sid "Sid, I need you to download some music for me" next up it's Blade "Blade please tell me you've got ye music coat on mush" "yow fuckin know it Davy boy, I neva leave home without it son." "ok guys, you and Sid are gona have to do some editing with the music ok" Brodi jumps in now "so come on Dave lad what's the plan then" "right, I think Sup is right, Sup can take someone and check out the other place super-fast and meet us at the building or club or whatever the fuck it is, we go in then all guns blazing on the cunts and I think I know a way to get H green again. it's all eyes on Dave as he gives a brief explanation "it's all to do with the music right, music's everything to H, some people just listen to music but H... H feels it an gets deep with it, it stirs him deep and he goes off, and that's where we need him, we need to get him to reminisce and then we get him angry, I don't know if it'll work but there's only one hope guys... music."

The Building 2009.

Spiderman's shiting it, he's fucking fuming, he keeps checking his little tv monitor, taping it to see if he can magic it back on, and to make things even worse the fucking boss is here asking him every five fucking minutes what they're doing. He's been telling lies for about two hours and he doesn't know how much longer he can keep it up, he's got fucking loads to do and to be honest he could do without the hassle. He's been over it in his head about a thousand times, what happened with his little bug? did it got too cold or hit a fan, he'd played the scene back a couple of times but you couldn't see much on the screen, one minute they're all boarding and the next poof, the screen of death. He's put his earphones on now to try block out Magneto's nagging and climbed up onto a machine to get out of his way.

Sabretooth has gone off to the furthest most part of the building working on things with his earphones on to block out the screams and moans of the people below, but poor Ra's is stuck right in the mix of things, fine tuning a little surprise by the front entrance with the poor screaming mortals just behind him. It had gotten worse throughout the day; these poor people had been tied up and unfed for days now. Nowhere to go and left to urinate and defecate in their own pants they were howling and absolutely fucking stinking, like a room of dead rats. A couple of them had already died and were left hanging from the rail, it was horrific and Ra's wanted no more of it.

As the screaming and moaning reaches fever pitch Magneto bubbles over, he storms across the room to the noisiest hostage and in one fluid movement slices the man's head from his body with a disc; the mans head rolls across the floor for the whole group to see and the LP shaped disk hovers malevolently, seeming to slightly vibrate with anger "if I hear one more whisper from here you will all suffer the same fate." Magneto storms off looking for Spiderman giving Ra's some peace again, he turns looking at the mortals and rubs his chin and cheeks in despair.

The Cave 2009.

Superman and Sid touch-down on a road circumventing a hilltop "well this is where the Audi was but" Sid turns in a full circle looking "there's fack-all here Sup" Superman though is looking at the huge rockface in front of them "that is the way in Sid, it is a loading bay" he scans the rest of the hill with his vision "it is a huge network of caves Sid, there is a better entrance on the top" he grabs Sid and shoots up BOOM; they land at the top and once again more rock, and once again Sid looks around hopelessly. Superman walks over to the rock and gives it a bang, and the rock swings open. As soon as the rock opened Sid could see clearly that it was just beat metal that looked like rock, but fuck me was it a good trick. Superman and Sid go quickly but stealthily through the cave system; they enter a room with a huge desk and hundreds of monitors. The two men try not take to much time but the monitors show everything; even this place, they can see the medical room where enchantress and the two wounded are and the building where all the others are going about their business, they note a few things about the building and its layout before moving on and as they get to the medical room its back to the old days. Sid goes in first stealth and invisible but comes out two seconds later "come on Sup, they're all facked to be honest" when Superman walks in the two men are asleep and hurt on beds and Enchantress is awake but in no fit state to put up any kind of a fight so the two men question her quickly.

Outside the Building 2009.

Superman and Sid touch-down opposite the building in an ally where all the rest of the gang are waiting "what's the scoop then Sup" asks Dave; Superman fills them in on the cave and what they found' he also fills them in on the layout of the building "right then I guess it's time" says Dave "I'll take Blade and Brian to the roof, they can enter from the top and the rest of us will take the front door" says Superman but Blade is already away shouting "no need Sup." Superman grabs Brian and swoops him to the top as Blade scales the building at lightning speed; he flips the parapet and lands on the roof as Superman touches down. The two men charge for the door as Superman takes off again flying down to meet the others at the door to the building, they all stand there for a moment with butterflies cursing through their bodies until Dave breaks the tension "come on guys lets fuck this place up" Superman nods smiling, he pushes the gang back showing off a little "stand back please" and BOOM he boots the door, and fuck all happens, but to be fair it's a big door and he only gives it a light kick "fuck sake Sup lad" says Dave, Superman mutters a sorry as he gives the door a proper kick.

Inside the Building 2009

Ra's has just finished at the door, he walks to the hostages and Magneto wrestling with his thoughts. He wants to ask Magneto to let them go but he knows he will lose his mind, he's getting worse and worse each day. As he reaches Magneto the boss turns looking at

Ra's smiling amid the tortured humans, but his smile turns to a frown when he sees Ra's expression; lucky for Ra's this is the moment that Superman throws a weak-ass kick at the door. The two men turn and look at the direction of the door "what the fuck was that" Magneto is looking at the contraption that Ra's had been working on thinking something had fallen, he turns to Ra's "did you set tha... BOOM, the front door... well it really just swings open and the gang march in as the door rebounds and closes behind them. at nearly exactly the same moment Blade and Brian come through a door at the top of the room and survey their surroundings. Spiderman working up high with his earphones on hadn't heard the door being kicked in but when the two fuckheads walked through the top door he was all eyes, he takes off his earphones and creeps along the metal trusses watching the two men and the new scene bellow. Blade and Brian immediately Know they are being watched and nod to each other, Blade goes one way and Brian goes the other, Spiderman watches the two men split and decides to follow that dirty fucking Wolverine thinking that Sabretooth can have the other. Sabretooth though is in a dark corner working when from the corner of his eye sees Spiderman creeping toward him, he spots more movement and steps back into the dark corner and watches Wolverine approach. Down below the gang march in and Superman takes centre stage "Magneto you wil..." Magneto clicks something and a huge metal net embraided with tiny diamonds of kryptonite lands on top of Superman pinning him to the floor screaming. "WHAT, sorry Kal-El I didn't hear that, did you say something Kal-El" mocks Magneto as he looks to the gang. Ra's can tell that Magneto is fuming it's too early, this is his plans all fucked, and he can see him scanning for Spiderman, he looks to Ra's "not to worry Ra's, a little change of plan that's all this is." The gang are on the floor trying to help Superman but to no avail really until they are brought back to reality by Magneto "right, your friends over there will die horrible deaths, OK, but if you comply with me it may be a little easier" he points to Dave "you bendy man come here" Dave reluctantly walks down the steps until he lands on the dancefloor, Magneto turns to Ra's "take him to the contraption." Ra's takes Dave and leads him to the side of the club where a strange huge chair-like contraption sits, he sits Dave down and as he starts to strap him in he whispers "I am sorry my friend, I do not want to be part of this, if there is some way I could help" Dave gives him a smile and a wink "it's ok mush you just crack on with your business, you'll know when to jump in kid if your serious" Ra's finishes tying Dave and walks back to the boss "it's time Ra's, wake the other two and let's get this show on the road. Ra's walks to the two bodies strapped down out cold and wafts something under their noses, they immediately come around "fuckinell, what the fuck" sputters H as he tries to take in his surroundings, the last he and Lysa knew they went to sleep soundly in H's bed. H looks down at the manacles holding him and then at Lysa who just tries to shrug, he looks around the room and sees Superman on the floor with a net over him and some of the gang trying to help, he turns and sees Dave trapped to a weird chair with both his arms out like Jesus and his legs strapped in weird cylinder like braces, then he hears the moaning of the hostages, He hears Magneto's voice before he sees him.

Brian walks along the top landing looking down at the scene below, he knows that whoever was following them took the bait and was still with him but he was ready feigning interest in the proceedings below, what he wasn't waiting for was the man mountain that came out of the shadows crushing him in a bear hold. Spiderman drops down in front of Brian "well hello stranger and how have we been all these years" Brian tilts his head "am sorry fella but I canny understand a fuckin word your sayin like, I see you still haven't grown a cock then" Sabretooth has to stifle a laugh as Spiderman goes mental "fucking let him go and well see whose dick-less. Sabretooth lets Brian go and CHING! Out come Wolverine's blades, three beautiful gleaming claws on each hand, Spiderman pulls two short Samurai from holders on his back and the two men... well one man, go right at it so hard that even Sabretooth has to step right back, it's just ching, ching, clash, clash, steel sparks flying everywhere.

Lysa who can usually get herself out of anything is fuming and quite scared now, she looks over at H "can you no change H" H looks over gutted shaking his head ashamed "no girl, I don't even want to try he'll just laugh. Magneto who had been babbling on barks in "YOU TWO, SHUT UP, I'm talking. Mel, crouching by Superman has had enough she stands and summons the storm, as she builds her energy, she hadn't noticed that the floor she's on is metal and as she channels that power straight into her body, BOOM she goes flying back into the doors. Magneto who was just chastising H and Lysa bursts into hysterical laughter "ooo it's fantastic to see you trying Marvellous but anybody else tries that shit and its death for you all. Magneto turns back to H and Sid immediately goes invisible and darts down the stairs creeping over sliding stealthily past Magneto to the manacles holding H and Lysa, but all he can do is sit and stare at the huge metal bracelets that would even baffle Houdini, he turns to Lysa but although they're only rope the knots are impossible to untie. Magneto takes a look at the motley crew by the door "no, on second thoughts you won't be good, I just know it, and you're to deviant, Emma" as he says the last words, he flicks his hand and two fat shards fly out and smash into Emma, one shoots into her hand and one smashes into her shoulder pinning her to the door. Brodi screams and runs to Emma desperately trying to free the shards. Magneto storms back over to H and Lysa "O how long I have waited for this, have you any idea what it's like, I despise you and your motley crew, but you Mr green man, you I hate the most, you I have desired to kill the most, but it wont be quick, o no, I'm going to make you suffer, your going to watch your friends die first, slowly and painfully." Magneto spits these last words out anger and rage cursing out from every pore; H sputters on the floor "fuckinell mush say it don't spray it ay, ye dirty bastard, spittin all over me there" Magneto bends to H and slaps him across the face "what" he slaps him again "did you just say something" he slaps him again harder "yes Mr incredible Hulk I'm slapping you like a girl" he slaps him again as hard as he can "like, slap, a, slap, little, slap, fucking, slap, crying, slap, girl, slap." Magneto turns to Ra's "I've had enough of this play talk, start that fucking machine" Ra's walks to the chair with Dave strapped in and presses a button on the side as Magneto scans the club; he's just about to ask Ra's about Sabretooth and Spiderman when he spies some sort of commotion from the upper levels. Magneto throws a tiny ball Bering to the floor, it hits it like a rain drop spreading out into a perfect disc, he walks on and lets the disc carry him up for a better view, a smile spreading across his face when he sees Spiderman and Wolverine going at it, Spiderman seeming to have the better hand with the two Samurai; he glides back down to H and Lysa "my good friend Spiderman has your wolf man beaten up there, your Super-buddy is lying dying under green gold, and that pathetic bitch just blew herself up Bahahaha, o glorious day, and now you get to watch this glorious show." The chair that Dave is sitting in starts to hum and the cylinders that hold Dave's arms and legs start to slowly rotate, Dave and H look at each other, Dave giving H that old smile and a little wink "it's ok big man" shouts down Dave "we've had some boss times me and you kid." The cylinders pick up a little speed and Dave's arms and legs start to ravel up winding like taffy in a sweet factory.

Spiderman throws a crashing blow at Brian that smashes into his blades, the final flick catching Brian across the cheek as the other comes up missing his chin by milometers. Blood seeps from Brian's cheek but the cut closes up instantly leaving the seeps to dry, Brian steps back breathing heavily. Fuck me this guy's good Brian's thinking, Spiderman seeming to read his thoughts "surprised are we wolf man, I have learnt a few skills over the years" he throws his blades to the floor "I don't even need these weapons for you, pathetic beast, he strides at Brian who holds his hand up confusing Spiderman for a second "am sorry like dick-less but as a said before like, a canny understand a fuckin word you say." Brian swipes upward with his blades but Spiderman has anticipated this, he catches Brian's arm in an Aikido hold on the way up and snaps it, the crunch and Brian's scream echoing around the club.

Dave hears Brian's scream and can't hold his own in, which in turn carries to H who lets out a frustrated roar of anger and hopelessness; Magneto lets out a roar of laughter which makes H even worse. H looks to Dave his friend in pain, at the poor humans tied up and then Lysa, he summons up all the anger inside like the days of old, he lets that white mist take over his mind, that rolling anger, nothing but the rage. H's eyes spring open as green as the valley and a flash of fear crosses Magneto's face, even Dave looks down amazed and excited, the sound of a huge rip echo's out around the club as H's big fat huge dick explodes from his pants. H roars in despair, anger and pure embarrassment as tears roll down his face, the rest of the gang's heads dropping, gutted. Magneto looks down at H revelling in the spectacle and then at Dave, twisted to almost breaking point "it's all over Marvellous, this is you..." Magneto is cut short by Dave who sits up in the chair struggling against his bonds "shut the fuck up bell-end" he looks up to the heavens and screams as loud as his lung will allow "REMENISS" and from up in the heavens the glorious music begins.

When Brian's arm snapped he retracted his blades and reverted to the martial arts he was so at ease with, switching styles every few moves to confuse Spiderman but the fucker was good and met every one of Brian's blows with ease and almost had him a few times with counter strikes. Brian feigns to throw a punch and instead swoops down for a leg sweep, Spiderman sees it coming a mile off and lets the move play out, reacting only when Brian is mid sweep. He crashes down on Brian's leg breaking it as another crack and scream echo's out.

Blade is in turmoil, perched on the metal trusses of the roof he looks down to the scene below, at H crying in despair, poor Emma pinned to the door, at Dave winding up like an elastic band, at Superman dying under the kryptonite net, at Mel unconscious and smoking and then at Brian battling away. Blade had wanted to swoop down, to save anyone, but he couldn't, he had to stay hidden, the crack of Brian's leg though becomes too much for Blade and he stands ready to jump to his friend's aid when he hears Dave scream those magic words.

Brian lies on the floor broken, bruised and bleeding as Spiderman walks over, he picks up a short blade and presses it to Brian's heart "do you think your immortality can take a blade through the heart, Brian looks up "your just mumblin mush, a canny hear a fuckin word" and in that instant a beautiful piano boom's out from above and Spiderman stupidly looks up. In one fluid beautiful movement Brian's blades shoot out and smack the sword away, his other hand slashing across and deep into Spiderman's leg, Spiderman's eyes for the first-time showing fear. Brian spins Wolverine-style arms out and sends his blades straight to Spiderman's heart, CHING, it's a weird paused moment in time with Brian's blades a hairs width from Spiderman's chest and Sabretooth's axe stopping them. Spiderman's face is a mixture of relief and surprise at the intervention of Sabretooth, a smile spreading across Spiderman's face as Brian crumbles, defeated. "thank you, my friend" mutters Spiderman to Sabretooth as he steps toward Brian "and now it really is time for you to die wolf man my friend here can do the honours beca..." from behind comes Sabretooth's beautiful gravel voice cutting off Spiderman "you misunderstand Dick-less, I wasn't going to let wolf boy here take the pleasure." Spiderman looks down at his other sword, (the one that he left on the floor) as it bursts slowly out of his chest covered in his own strange blood. Sabretooth grabs Spiderman's shoulders for extra purchase and shoves a little harder; whispering in Spiderman's ear "I told you I would rip your fucking head off" and in one fluid graceful movement Sabretooth pulls the blade from Spiderman's torso, spins and takes off Spiderman's head. DUM, DUM, DUM, it rolls toward Brian who scuttles backward "eeeee fuckinell man that's fuckin gross like" Sabretooth, hands out waving all apologetic gives the head a boot and offers Brian his hand "err sorry about that, always hated that fucking rat."

Blade presses the button on his MP3 player and listens to the first notes as he watches Brian spinning in full Wolverine mode smacking Spiderman's sword away but then he nearly has a heart attack thinking his friend is going to die, but when Sabretooth saves the day, he runs across the trusses Blade style as if on solid ground and swoops down to join Brian.

Ra's hears the music start and looks around confused; he looks at Magneto who also looks confused; he watches Magneto looking around and then laughing "its just music, fucking music." Ra's looks over at Mr Fantastic, a twisted mess barely recognisable; Ra's can't take this anymore, he runs at the machine arm out finger poised to press the stop button until he sees the shard, and hears Magneto.

Magneto hears Dave scream and a bolt of fear and confusion runs through him for a second as the music starts; Magneto thinking he'd missed something or there was some super plan he'd not predicted. It's just music he's thinking, he even shouts it to Ra's, "its just music, fucking music." Its then that he's betrayed, he feels like he's been shot through the heart like Jon Bon Jovi as his long-time friend Ra's races for the chair, finger out darting for the stop button. Magneto, furious at the betrayal launches a metal shard, it flies around stopping inches from Ra's face "so it has come to this then, betrayed by my own friend" "this has gone too far Magneto, those humans down there don't deserve this, and these men and women here we don't even know anymore, they're strangers to us" "you week minded fool you…" just at that moment a big wet football splats down and rolls past Magneto knocking him off his train of thought, and everybody's eyes follow the weird football until it comes to rest and we finally see Spiderman's gross black dead eyes staring up at us. As Magneto's attention is taken the metal shard falls and Ra's bounds for the button smashing it sending the machine to a halt; he dives behind a podium. Magneto turns, his fury reaching critical mass, he watches Spiderman's head rocking to a stop, sees his friend Ra's smash the button and then hears the Hulk scream for his friend, crying like a baby. It's then that Dave screams again, yes, from somewhere in the twisted mess that Dave is he somehow finds the will and way to pop his lips out and scream, "GREEN BABY, SEND THE PAIN."

Blade, still up in the rafters hears the call and pushes the button.

H is lying in his contraption and he's never felt so useless, everyone was about to die and all he could do was grow a dick. Tears roll down his cheeks as every last bit of hope is drained from his mind. Its then that he hears Dave scream, the next thing H knew he was in heaven as one of the most amazing songs in history (as far as H was concerned) boomed from out of nowhere. A beautiful piano explodes into H's brain, the amazing My Immortal by Evanescence drags H down out of the room, out of the misery and into bliss pure reminiscing bliss, and when Amy Lee's voice cuts in, WOOH. "I'm so tired of being here, suppressed by all my childish fears, and if you have to leave" H is gone, in the past he and Dave at rave's bopping, at Glastonbury, at a Doors gig, watching the Beatles, shagging two birds and high five'ing each other, getting stoned, pissed, E'd up, fighting, kissing, hugging, singing, dancing. A huge swell of emotion surges through H like a wave on Fistral beach, riding through him, a wave of pure brotherly love and as the song reaches the climax H cries out to his friend, and his friend answers his call. H is furious, there he was enjoying himself, drifting along in a beautiful dream and the next thing, BER BEM, BUR BEM, a nasty fat evil grungy guitar pounds over his beautiful melody destroying his memories and dragging him into the present, into that evil horrid place, but the song, the song, evil, heavy with feeling, pounding into him is Limp Bizkit's Break Stuff telling him that everything is fucked and everybody fucking sucks, and H is feeling it, letting that raw evil ferocious anger build like never before, letting those memories from before come back and intertwine with the anger, with the rage with that unstoppable ferocious green anger, and when Fred reaches the climax, when he builds it up to that glorious peak, the raw thunderous moment of "GIVE ME SOMTHIN TO BREAK" H's eyes spring open like Arnie in Total Recall at the end when he's got no air, bright fucking green.

Magneto watches the head of his friend Spiderman roll past and then watches his treacherous bastard friend Ra's stop the chair, he hears the Hulk screaming like a baby and his friend in return, he watches it all like a sick perverted dream where everything was going wrong, not wanting to believe what his eyes where telling him, but it was real, as real as the anger in his belly, as real as the rage in his heart. Magneto roars in fury "COME OUT FROM THERE RA'S AL GHUL, YOU FUCKING TRAITOR" Ra's steps out from behind the podium to face Magneto with Fred Durst booming from somewhere above. Magneto shakes his head as he looks at Ra's gesticulating wildly with is hands "what is this fucking god awful racket, fucking music, music, what, you think you can kill me with music, fucking heavy metal" Ra's walks over to the machine completely ignoring Magneto and puts the machine in reverse unravelling Dave; Sid on the floor spots this and dives over to Dave to try and help him out "what the fuck are you doing Ra's" shouts Magneto "it's over Magneto, it' over" "I say when it's over, I say when it's done, if Enchantress where here, fuck you Ra's fuck you all" Magneto raises a shit-load of metal turning them into tiny shards pointing them at Dave and Ra's, but Ra's looks calmly into Magnetos eyes "Magneto my friend it isn't us you should be worried about, it's him" Ra's points back across Magneto's shoulder to the forgotten H and Lysa lying in their contraptions. H isn't green but his head is in spasms from side to side and every vein in his body throbbing and growing. Magnetos eyes narrow as he forgets about the others and turns at H wondering whether he should use his mind control drugs now, but Fred has started the build and H is listening "I hope you know I pack a chainsaw, I'll skin ya ass raw" as Magneto gets closer to H with his shards all around him he watches the beast twitching all over with little spasms, breathing rapidly and sweating like a cross trainer, Fred winding him up, "and if my day keeps goin this way I might just break somthin tonight" Magneto starts to panic and backs off slightly but it's too late "and if my day keeps goin this way I might just break your fuckin face tonight, the Bizkit hit it and the club explodes with monstrous sound "GIVE ME SOMTHIN TO BREAK" H's eyes spring open the most glorious colour green and he roars the most spectacular roar right in Magnetos face as every muscle in his body rapidly starts to explode turning the most glorious green as it pops and rips, Fred surges on "GIVE ME SOMTHIN TO BREAK" H's shackles explode as he grows, he rips the other shackle throwing it roaring, growing all the time humongous green "HOW BOUT YOUR FUCKING FACE" Magneto, terrified turns to run but Hulk is out now standing huge roaring and leaps Hulk style RRRRAAAAHHHHHH. He lands at Magnetos back grabbing him like an action man doll throwing him to the ground and with Fred in the background supplying the soundtrack H ground and pounds that motherfucker UFC style to dust. "GIVE" BOOM, "ME" BOOM, "SOMETHIN" BOOM, "TO" BOOM, "BREAK" POUND, POUND, BOOM, BOOM LEFT, RIGHT, LEFT, RIGHT, LEFT, RIGHT, BOOM, "HOW" BOOM, "BOUT" POUND, "YOUR" BASH, "FUCKING" BOOM, "FACE" LEFT, RIGHT, LEFT, RIGHT, BOOM, BOOM, BOOM, BOOM, BOOM. H doesn't stop he pounds and pounds into the face of Magneto and then turns to his body stomping pounding smashing ripping and roaring until there's nothing but a pile of mush and rubble blood and guts. All the gang are here now watching eyes wide mesmerised; Mel had recovered and gone back to help Superman, and with magneto's hold on the metal diminishing with the distractions she's able to drag the mesh blanket off, the two of them now lay on the floor watching the show. Blade, Brian and Sabretooth had come down from the rafters and were standing above watching, when H took over the situation they ran to the humans to help them out, undoing them from their shackles and trying to sit them comfortably until they could get them help, Blade turning off the music once H had finished.

Brodi didn't do anything to be fair when Emma got pinned he did all he could to free her and when Magneto's attention faltered and the shards came loose all he wanted to do was help her and heal her, and to be fair for a minute there it looked like they were all fucked anyhow. Sid had materialised when it all went off and he and Ra's had been helping Dave, they had rewound the machine but had to do it very slowly as Dave tried to pull himself back together. Poor Lysa was still lying in the traps on the floor, but to be honest, every single one of them no matter what state they were in, were glued like shit to the show that H had just put on, exploding out his humongous shackles growing bigger than ever before, gigantic naked green monster leaping and grabbing Magneto and pounding him none stop until nothing but pulp remained. They all stand there now staring at H, H still gigantic green, breathing heavy looking down at the pulp, covered in the pulp, the pulp dripping from his monstrous arms. He snorts loudly and shakes his head as if just shaking off a dream and looks around the rom at everyone, and each person he looks at cowers back or looks away. Superman looks at Mel and tries to get up but Mel grabs his arm and whispers "don't be stupid, your too weak, he'll tear you to pieces." Blade and the lads carry on looking after the humans but watching H precariously, luckily most of the humans had their backs to the spectacle that had just unfolded, but I imagine anyone they told the story to anyhow would think they were crackers. Dave tries to sit up "help me sit up lads and I'll calm him down, am the only one who can, he'll fuckin tear dis place apart if I don't." Lysa looks up at H, and H looks down at Lysa, huge green rippling beast, he takes two huge strides toward her, the room seeming to rumble and Lysa lets out a tiny scream, the rest of the room holds its breath collectively. The Hulk's brow furrows, huge eyebrows coming together, he looks around the room at everyone one more time and then he bends toward Lysa his huge hands outstretched and the little voice of H comes out "I don't know what the fuck's up wid all youse, you'd think you'd seen a fuckin ghost or sumthin" he snaps the ropes off Lysa and swoops her out of the contraption and tries to nuzzle his humongous head into her neck "wow there ya fuckin wee big galloot, remember how big ye fuckin are" H starts laughing "sorry girl just glad you're ok babe." The whole gang do a collective sigh of relief and carry on with things. H carries Lysa over to Dave and the lads who are still trying to unravel Dave. Brodi, having removed the shards from Emma and rapped her wounds, witch where healing quite quickly, picks her up and carries her over to the gang. Blade and Brian had been helping Ra's and Sabretooth with the humans carrying them to the van outside, Ra's thanks the two men "we will take them to the hospital and meet you all later at the manor to talk about the Enchantress and the other two, and also to explain ourselves, but let us help these people first." Sabretooth takes the van and Ra's jumps into H's Audi wheel-spinning off and fishtailing the back-end like a lunatic, Brian turns to Blade as they go back in to see the others "do ya think Ra's knows that he's joy-ridin in the fuckin Hulks Audi like" Blade has a little chuckle as he thinks about it. They re-enter the building just after Brodi had picked Emma up, they help Mel and Superman and follow them over to the gang. Dave's head's looking quite normal now and he's chatting away to the lads as they slowly unravel his body. They all stand there looking at H with wonder in their eyes, H laughs "fuckinell, youse was all shit scared of me before" the gang are all pissing themselves and Blade asks Dave "how did yow know that H would change when he heard them songs Davey lad" "well, I didn't really kid, it's just that every time he listened to My Immortal he'd cry his fuckin eyes out, cry like a fuckin little kid he would" H is laughing, he points a fucking huge finger at Dave "alright, alright bollocks the fuckin Hulk don't cry alright" Dave carries on "so ye, an then that

Limp Bizkit song fuckin Break stuff, fuckinell, I had to fuckin ban that shit, I saw him once, caught him just in time I did fuckin eyes green, fuckin veins bubblin just about to fuckin change I swear, there's been some other times over the years so I knew he was in there somewhere so I kind of thought that those two songs put together would do the trick, I wasn't wrong ay guys" the whole gang turn and look up at the man mountain The Hulk and Dave speaks up "I don't understand kid, where is he? Where's the big man?" the whole gang are nodding confused but H just smiles a fucking huge Hulk smile "the big man got bored and fed up of watchin life through my eyes, got fuckin fed up of only comin out when I needed him so he just kind of went to sleep, I can still feel him there but he's sleepin, I only turn green if I'm really gona die" "so how come you could Hulk you dick out" "well he can probably still feel it in his sleep cant he, and ye not gona fuckin knock that back are ye, it's got us a fair bit o pussy over the years hasn't it mush" Dave's nodding away, huge smile on his face "o yer it certainly has big man, it fucking certainly has" Lysa standing next to H looks up at him "how long are ye ganny be like that then" "err, I don't know to be fair girl, probably a few hours" Emma croaks up "let's get out of here then guys, it's fucking horrible, let's get back to the manor" the gang all nod and start helping each other walk out, H hilariously helps Superman by pinching the back of his suit and holding him, making him look like he's on a clothes line "thanks for your help there Sup lad" says H as they walk out "couldn't of done it without you lad" Superman head bowed down looking gutted shakes his head "listen Sup lad you was the shit mush I swear, the way ye just lied on the floor mush, it was fuckin brilliant, couldn't of done it without ye, it was amazin, the next time I need someone to lie on the floor like that mush you're the fuckin man, I've never seen anyone lie on the floor like that before" Superman turns to H still shaking his head but a fabulous smile spreading across his face "shut the fuck up bollocks" H is pissing himself as he gives Superman a big hug "that's more like it, that's the Super mush I know and love." the gang had all been listening and are loving the banter, walking out all in good spirits as they leave the building. It looks like a scene from a movie as they all come out in a line, some limping being helped by others some swaggering. Blade had given H his coat to hide his bits and pieces and they looked cool as fuck, and then H swaggering gives Brian a little matey tap on the shoulder, but forgets he's the Hulk and Brian trips over, he does a little run trying to keep himself up but eventually hits the fucking tarmac and all the gang are pissing themselves pointing, H picks him up dusting him off. "sorry Bri don't know me own strength kid."

The manor 2009.

As the cars roll back onto the driveway of the manor popping and pinging on the gravel Superman touches down with the big man H and his best mucka Dave, (the big fucker H wouldn't fit in any cars and Dave, having nearly pulled himself back together just wanted to fly) H is already starting to recede in his girth and some of that fabulous emerald green starting to fade and make him look a sickly grey-green. H's forehead and eyebrows immediately scrunch up and his head swivels around the carpark like a meercat "where the fuck's me car? As some cunt robbed my car?" "O yer kid" says Dave as he stretches an arm around the big man, "forgot to tell you that some cunt robbed ye car" H, shaking his head "yer well, who fuckin was it then" "haven't got a fuckin clue kid, it was just gone when we got up the other day, we thought at first you'd gone out in it" the other cars have pulled into their spaces and the guys are already piling out, H has his hands out in a wonderous pleading gesture "come on guys someone must know, who the fuck robbed me car?" most of the gang are giggling as they depart the vehicles and start to pile back into the manor shrugging and holding their own hands out to H in their own little gestures of I aint got a clue. Blade and Brian come walking over to H from the Aston Martin, Brian had taken Dave's place for the ride back in the X6, Blade tries to put his hand on H's shoulder but it's still way to high so decides just to give his huge bicep a slap "we don't know who took your car from here H but the last time we saw it Ra's al Ghul was fuckin throwing it all over the place, said he's gona bring it back here though, soon as they've dropped all the poor fuckers off at the hospital" Brian and Blade had taken stride at either side of the big man as he looks down at them "O fuckin did he ye, well if there's even a fuckin dust spec on it, the cunts getting filled in." the gang march back into the manor and H heads straight for the kitchen taking great care around the doorways for some glorious coffee. The rest of the gang head straight for the big comfy couches, most of them start to skin up for some well earned doobage as they rest their weary limbs and let their wounds heal. The room's pretty quiet at first with everybody finding their things and bearings, but once everyone's settled and skinning up the conversation and chatter starts. At first, it's a few "I had a feeling or I knew it was going to be them" and then the scars start to get compared until the room's suddenly filled with shouting and laughter as fifteen conversations try to outshout each other. As H manoeuvres his way out of the kitchen with a huge tray filled with mugs and two huge urns of coffee, sugars and what not, he looks out of the window to see Ra's and the Audi come flying up the driveway in a hail of dust, Ra's does a huge handbreak turn into the empty spot. The doors to the Audi open and the comical huge frames of Ra's and Sabretooth exit the tiny Audi. All the gang had paused for a moment looking out of the window to watch the Audi show, but they all turn now looking at the weird, still huge, but shrinking grey-green figure of H holding the tray and eyebrows raise all around the room "cheeky cunt, fuckin see that" says H "with my fuckin Audi, right" H sends a little smile around the gang, "let's have some fun ay." Ra's and Sabretooth look like a pair of school boys heading for the headmaster's office as they walk toward the front door of the manor. Brian jumps up and runs for the front door to let the newcomers in and after a bit of muffling Ra's and Sabretooth walk through to the communal room to meet the gang. The first thing or even sound that the two men are greeted with is H's scouse accent "did you fuckin rob my fuckin Audi" H's huge finger points at Ra's face and Ra's turns the colour of boiled shit "err, no Mr Hulk I most certainly did not, that would have been Spiderman" Ra's looks around the solemn faces of the gang who are giving nothing away and finds Brian; points his finger "and I do believe he killed him for you." Ra's smiles at H but it soon disappears as H roars again "I fuckin seen you drive in like a fuckin loon, did you scratch my car?" H points his finger between the two men now, looking at them both and even the huge frame of Sabretooth shrinks a little but Ra's cracks on "no Mr Hulk I did not, my driving skills are sublime, if there is a scratch it would have been done by that nasty bastard Spiderman." H can't help himself and he bursts out laughing and the gang join in "HA HAA am only kiddin lads come on, come in an get yoursens a seat." The two men take a little sigh of relief each and take seats in the communal room and within a few seconds are handed (to their delight) a joint each. H stars asking everyone what the have their coffee like and starts dishing it out and once again not before long there's a shitload of shouting, laughing, screaming going on. Ra's and Sabretooth start to try and explain themselves a little but to be fair the gang aren't really arsed and tell them to chill the fuck out, "it'll all get sorted out in the next few weeks lads, don't worry about it" says Dave, but to be fair it kind of gets sorted out right here right now because for the rest of the night the gang heal, get stoned and drunk and sort out what's happening with all the shit.

Superman and Ra's have been gabbing and they're going to look after the cave and the others, they're going to give them a chance at living normal and see how it goes, but Ra's has serious reservations about Enchantress saying she's a lot like Magneto in her ways. They're also going to go to the club and clean it up for selling. Superman tells the gang he's going to monitor the government and army now to see what and how much they really know and also to make sure none of the gang are in danger, he's also going to look for missing members and others they all knew like Wonder woman. H buts in here getting the whole gangs attention "listen gang, we've had a fuckin mad fuckin day an we all need a little chillout day an a little bonding, an I know the perfect fuckin thing for it, fuckin race track day" H looks around the room with a huge grin "come on gang, tomorrow let's all go race ar cars, come on" all the gang are laughing now, some of them saying yes "are you sure you'll be back to normal by tomorrow" asks Emma "too fuckin right I will if its fuckin race day, come on gang" most of the gang give in and agree. Brian and Sabretooth have been getting on like a house on fire and Brian's even invited him to stay at his for a while when they leave, but the gang as a whole have decided to stay for a few weeks more to catch up and really get to know each other, and as the night crawls on its good times all round with the drinks coming out and more joints being built, plans are laid and more friendships are made.

The next morning the gang are all up early. H bounds down the stairs into the communal room looking his good old self in an old Waterboys t-shirt "now then motherfuckers who's up for fuckin race day" most of the guys are up and lounging around on the couches but all seem up for it and this send H's excitement levels through the roof " fuckin spot on mushes, Sid come on kid do us a favour an dive on the net see if ye can sort us a track somewhere, nice one mush am off the kitchen guys, full fuckin breaky all round for me muckers" when H leaves Sid grabs his laptop and starts to look, and the gang have a little nervous chat about going to a race track "it'll be fine kids" sooths Dave "we've been loads of times ye don't av to go fast if ye don't want to" Emma buts in though " I think we're more worried about our cars Dave, how good is H's driving and can he be trusted with our cars" "let me tell ye girl there's nothin to be worried about with H at the wheel he's a fuckin top jockey is H" Brian joins Dave now "al have to admit Emma, H is pretty fuckin good behind the wheel like, but to be honest guys I won't be goin anyhow, a canny be assed today like but ye can take my car if ye want Davy lad" Emma also spoils the party by saying she also doesn't want to go, Brodi's absolutely gutted as he wanted to have a blast at the Bugatti but Emma knows and tells him to go enjoy himself. H comes back in and to his delight Sid tells him that he's been able to secure a small private track for the day "it's gona fackin cost though mate, al tell yer that" "don't you fuckin worry about tha Sid lad me an Dave are fuckin loaded we're fuckin payin for this" H then tells the gang to get their asses into the kitchen for breaky while they sort out who's going and who's driving what, it's only Sabretooth Wolverine and Emma who decide not to go really, and sadly that's where we leave the gang, planning the perfect day out at the race track with a set of the most amazing vehicles in the world.

Leaving day 2009.

Its leaving day for some of the gang, and sadly to say we're leaving with them, H and Lysa are off snowboarding and Dave's heading back to Liverpool, most of the gang have decided to move to the manor for now so Dave's off to Liverpool to pack up their gear and move it down. Dave didn't mind doing it on his own as H is going to Lysa's on the way back from snowboarding to help her down to the manor.

Emma and Brodi are off to Surf some giant waves somewhere first, saying they're moving when they get back. The rest of the gang are split helping each other with their moves, Sabretooth going with Mel and the three lads Blade, Brian and Sid are all going to follow each other to their respected properties. Ra's and Superman have done an amazing job with the cave turning it into a superhero control room just in case anybody fancied getting into the old game and it's partly the reason that everyone's decided to move, they've also converted the cells down below into amazing rehab centre for lost fucked up old super whatever's or fucked up humans. Enchantress is down there in her own private luxury cell, Ra's being right about her not wanting to become part of society. And the others are healing also in their own private wards. So, the gang are all outside hugging and kissing and high fiveing and fist bumping and wishing each other luck, telling each other they'll see one another soon, as we glide off away from the manor watching them walk on the dusty gravel to their cars.

Outro.

Not many news reports or newspapers spoke about the events that came to pass a few weeks ago and none of the hostages would speak out about what happened (Superman would keep his eye on this situation) only one person was rambling about what happened and that was from the care centre he had been admitted to. There was a report about women, lots of women that had been given huge anonymous donations into their bank accounts and none of them knew why, and a story about two American extreme snowboarders deep in the arctic who said they heard a man and a woman screaming for help, they searched the mountain for a day but since nobody had been reported missing they called it off.

Karaoke night 2009.

It's late and deep into karaoke night and Brian's taken the knock, Dave and H are hovering, whispering and planning. Dave thinks they might be going too far but H is saying come on mush he can take it he heals up super-fast. Dave and H take a hand each and make a fist placing it on Brian's chest just under his chin and then Dave steps back. Most of the gang have been watching intrigued and now they're gathered around for the grand finale. H stand straight in front of Brian and gives the biggest roar he possibly can, Brian wakes screaming Wolverine style springing his blades straight into his chin and jaw; he sits for a moment gurgling the whole gang sit transfixed like that scene in Pulp Fiction with the syringe until Brian retracts his blades fuming "you're a pair of evil fucking bastards, fuck me pet that hurt like."

On the way to the skate park 2009.

Were on a beautiful English country road or it would be beautiful but for the roar of an engine as Brian's amazing Aston Martin comes racing toward us. As it passes we dive into the back window and take a seat for the ride, H is fucking bombing it through the country lanes and brain's screaming like a child on a roller-coaster "come on Bri lad calm yeself mush, top fucken jockey me Bri" "O please H please slow doon, ye gona scratch me baby" H is still screaming down the country lanes as he looks at Brian shaking his head "am insulted mush I've never scratched a car in me life" as H turns back to the road he spots the mini roundabout up ahead, takes a look at Brian and smiles, then puts the pedal to the fucking metal, fucking boooooom, Brian lets out a pleading scream as he notices the roundabout but H is flying and not letting up, the roundabout comes up at the boys in lightning speed an H takes that motherfucker like Mansell on a fifty bag of Ching. As they come out of H's amazing manoeuvre around the roundabout H looks across to Brian whose staring at H with tears in his eyes shaking, his hands stretched out and his huge gleaming blades thrust into the beautiful dashboard of his Aston Martin DB9, H shakes his head "what the fuck ye do that for, fuckin slashin up yer own car, fuckin madness mate."

The end.

Thank you, cynical J.

Printed in Poland
by Amazon Fulfillment
Poland Sp. z o.o., Wrocław